Survival Prose

An Anthology of New Writings

Survival Prose

An Anthology of New Writings

edited by John Bart Gerald and George Blecher
with an introduction by Seymour Krim

The Bobbs-Merrill Company, Inc.
Indianapolis / New York

The Bobbs-Merrill Company, Inc.
A Subsidiary of Howard W. Sams & Co., Inc.
Publishers / Indianapolis • New York • Kansas City

Copyright © 1971 by The Bobbs-Merrill Company, Inc.
Library of Congress catalog card number 78-142468

Design by Quentin Fiore

The editors gratefully acknowledge permission to reprint
"When State Magicians Fail," which originally appeared in
Syracuse Nickel Review.

This anthology presents fifteen fiction-writers. Many of us are new and unpublished; some have published novels, short stories or articles. Some of us are in our twenties; some are a good deal older. We do not want to represent a movement or revolutionary "generation" of writers with similar styles and points of view. But there is something which we all hold in common: we are each committed to making some difficult, hard-earned sense out of life as we discover it in a time when slogans and easy generalizations have become increasingly attractive.

As collectors and editors of this cooperative anthology, we would like to thank Seymour Krim for his help and advice, and the St. Mark's Fiction Workshop, where much of this material was first read.

New York, N.Y.   J. B. G.

                                                      G. B.

Contents

Introduction

The St. Mark's Fiction Workshop, where I gave and took as older-type umpire once a week from 1967 to 1969, was the wildest place of its kind I've ever heard of. Buried down in the Lower East Side like some kind of embarrassing secret, we argued, yelled, confronted, got white, bled internally, laughed obnoxiously and all the rest of it right through the year. Each session was a psychic workout that left me a wreck afterwards, even the coolest of them. I had come down as literary traffic cop, umpire, keep-it-together man, call it what you will, after doing a similar job at Columbia University's School of General Studies but that was child's play compared to this weekly plunge into the unknown. No one was safe—visiting writers, myself, oldtimers, newcomers, it made no difference. Reputations were crap compared to what you could deliver. And it was on the basis of delivering that new reputations were made; some of them you'll recognize in these pages, others like Shulamith Firestone, M. G. Stephens, Jerry Roth (Joth), Frances Starr, Arnold Swiller, etc. are not here but like their peers you'll doubtless be hearing from them too if you haven't already done so. We were an active bunch, if only out of cosmic self-defense, and out of our activity work came spurting like matter from long-suppressed wounds. Theoretical, yes, we faced each other down with individual visions of what the hell literature should be today; but it was in action that we stamped ourselves and it was literary action—getting published, getting to other heads—that became our goal. I know such a goal can be overdone but can say without guilt that I emphasized publishing from the first night that I stepped into the St. Mark's ring; not publishing at any price, but ALMOST any price, because when all the talk and self-justification is over it is only your words in print that justify your calling yourself a writer. And I'm proud and competitive enough to say that our group began, one way and another, to publish like desperados, to the point that their old Punching Bag has been put nicely uptight by this combined threat to use up all the available space and drive him into oblivion. Go! May the better writer collect the minds out there! And may the reader, the brain-sogged American consumer of words, benefit from this rush to jab an urgent message into your head and make you respond. We were a driven gang and very much New York in our pace, style, harshness, humor. This kind of "survival prose," as co-editor Bart Gerald coined it in a right-on moment of superior truth, could only have come off the gunpoint New York streets. I don't necessarily mean gunpoint literally, although members of our group were not unfamiliar with weapons and their cold-touch reality, but I do mean life-death situations where your future was a gambler's chance and tomorrow only a fantasy. But you'll see this in the work. It is rawnerved mostly, as exposed and strident as we were towards each other in the weekly confrontations that both stripped and re-energized us. Although the individuals you'll meet in these pages, the writers, will separate themselves as the years go by —deep needs will drive a mysterious handful further and harder than others, so goes the justice of injustice—what you have before you is really the expression of a small society, a literary commune, which will never be repeated. Efforts have been made to reconstitute the Workshop, bind the living parts into a whole once again, but changes in our own lives have cast us upon other possibilities of the exhausting American dream and it's doubtful if we'll ever pick up where we left off. New communes of writers will produce new and different shared experience, but we New York sidewalk braves and sisters of the late 60s have had to go it alone now with the breakup of our tribe. I was older than all the others, sometimes by as much as 25 years, but I needed them to show me the light when I had lost the sight of it. All writing is concerned finally with light, even the blackest, and here is hard new light for you and I feel it flickering all around me once again as I make way for those who have earned the right to give you their, our, understanding of light.

SEYMOUR KRIM
The Writer's Workshop
Iowa City, Iowa
December 10, 1970

Clark Whelton

James Purcell

Through the cold, wet days near the end of winter, Mary Purcell formed a dream of her husband's death. Cautiously, but with increasing confidence, like someone who has had success with shoplifting, she arranged and rearranged the details until at last they seemed to fit together correctly. It would be an accident. His automobile would take him to a far place, there would be an accident and someone else would be responsible for the body. Their home would be unmarked by memories of his dying. Her life would begin again. In the long afternoons, while her daughter napped, she often walked through the dusky house, adjusting the furniture and changing the newspaper that protected the carpets. Sometimes she just stood among the silent machines in the kitchen, watching the sparrows on the snow outside. And each day her dream became clearer until her husband's return from the city at sundown would occasionally come as a surprise.

In the spring her brother-in-law, a lawyer in a nearby town, was convicted of non-payment of seven years' income tax. There was hope that he would not go to prison since he had already paid the back taxes, penalties and interest and

CLARK WHELTON is a freelance writer. His articles appear frequently in the *Village Voice*.

had friends in the legislature. On the day that he was to be sentenced, Mary Purcell and her husband and daughter were driving to be in the courtroom. They had been on the road for a short time when two men in a station wagon ran through a stop sign and into the path of their car. Mary Purcell screamed a warning and her husband whirled the steering wheel to the right. For a moment it appeared that they would not leave the pavement, but as he spun the wheel back again the car swerved, turned over and rolled down an embankment. Mary Purcell was still conscious when the car stopped moving. She realized that she was upside down in the twisted metal and that water was seeping in through the shattered windshield. Turning slightly, she saw her daughter lying across the ceiling light. She reached out to touch her, but her arm would not move in the right direction.

"It looks like just the concussion," the doctor who examined James Purcell said. "And the gravel they picked out of his back. Thrown out on the first flip."

"Lucky," a hospital administrator said.

"And you still use your seat belt?"

"I'll play the percentages," the administrator said.

They waited two days after the blood had stopped trickling from James Purcell's ears to tell him that his family was dead. He struggled to sit up. "No," he said in a low voice. "No. Did my little girl see my wife dead?"

"Steady now," the doctor said, easing him back to the pillow. "Steady." He took Purcell's left wrist between his fingers. Purcell turned his head to one side and covered his eyes with the other wrist. "Mary," he said in the same low voice. "Mary, Mary."

When Purcell was released from the hospital, his wife's family had already arranged for the funeral and the formalities had been completed. Several days later many of his friends came to his house. He brought some liquor down from the attic. As he was walking toward the kitchen he heard one of his neighbors say: "You see how important wills are? Today, everything's fine. Tomorrow, bingo! And I'll tell you, life insurance for women is something to think about."

"The trick is knowing when to insure them," a voice answered.

When everyone had gone, Purcell paced back and forth behind the living room drapes, gently rubbing the bandage attached to the shaven spot on his scalp. Then he locked the front and back doors. In the back hallway he noticed that someone had taken the newspapers from the steps every day while he was in the hospital and had stacked them in two neat piles on a shelf next to his daughter's roller skates. He carried both piles to the kitchen table. On the front page of one paper was a picture of his brother in handcuffs being led from the Federal Building. "Prominent Attorney Gets Nine Months In Tax Case" the headline read. On page three he saw a picture of his car lying on its roof in a drainage ditch. He tore the page from the paper, crumpled it and threw it across the room. But after he had dropped the other papers in the trash barrel, he came back into the kitchen, picked up the page and smoothed out the wrinkles. Near the end of the article about the accident he read that his wife had been coughing up blood when she was removed from the car. He stood up, knocking his chair to the floor. "Why the hell did they put that in the paper?" he said, his voice weaving among the highball glasses his friends had left near the sink. "What do they expect? What could I do?"

Two days later his brother's wife, Phyllis, came by in the evening. She had been to the prison to leave a package for her husband. Visitors were not permitted during the first month. "He's not going to appeal," she said. "He wants to serve his time and get it over with." She began to cry. "I don't know why they had to put him in there. He paid them their damn money and that's what it's all about, isn't it? I'm the one who's suffering now." As she went to the sink for a paper towel she saw the glasses. "Promise me you won't drink too much, Jim," she said. "Please, promise me that."

On Saturday morning the man who drove James Purcell to the station came in through the garage carrying his golf clubs. Purcell told him what the paper had written about the accident, and said: "I'll get them for that."

3

The man shook his head. "Why feel that way about it?" he said. "I've been reading that paper for a long time and lately they feel that they have to report certain details to keep their circulation up. It's simply a question of ad lineage. It would be a mistake to take it personally." As he talked he picked up the glasses one by one and rinsed them under cold water. "Come on," he said. "You're hanging around the house too much. Get outside. Let's play nine holes."

In June the shaven spot on Purcell's head was no longer visible and he decided to buy a car. On weekends and during his lunch hour in the city he went to the different showrooms. "No trade-in," he had to say at each one. At the end of the month he bought a metallic blue Porsche, second-hand but in almost new condition.

"This car was broken in right," the dealer told him. "You know how important that is for a good engine."

The next day Purcell left the house early and drove all the way to the city. After work he returned home by a longer route, arriving well after dark. "This is the car," he thought. "It's what I should have had all along."

Purcell took the car to work each morning. He learned how to handle the gearbox, brakes and steering. One Sunday he drove two hundred and fifty miles, almost running out of gas because he hadn't wanted to stop the engine. When he finally pulled into a service station the attendant patted one of the fenders and asked: "Do you race her?"

As he turned into his driveway that night he saw his brother's car parked in the shadows by the garage. His sister-in-law was halfway down the stairs when he turned on the light in the front hall. He could smell the liquor on her breath. "Where have you been?" she asked. "I was worried."

"How did you get in?"

"You left the door open. You should be more careful." She reached out to steady herself against his arm.

"Are you alone?" he asked.

"Of course I'm alone. Do you think I bring my lovers here?"

"That's not what I meant."

"Yes it is. That's what all men mean." She looked up at him, squinting into the bright light above his head. "And where have you been so late? Who have . . . whose little . . ." She tried to toss her head but lost her balance, lurched backwards and sat down hard on the bottom step. Her hair fell across her face.

"I'm sorry, Jim. Really, I am. It's just that everything has been so awful, so goddamned awful. The children have to go back to public school, the bank is opening some kind of an investigation into our account and I hardly have enough money for food let alone for myself, and Stuart won't be home for months and months." She began to sob. "You must miss her so much. Your poor wife and beautiful little daughter dead and buried in another state. It's so awful. When you get used to reaching out at night and touching someone and then they're not there any more. It's just so awful."

After she left, Purcell turned off the lights, locked the door behind him and drove the Porsche up into the hills beyond the town. The cool night air blew down the front of his shirt and up the legs of his trousers.

"Upstate on weekends," the dealer who had sold him the car said. "You can race during the week too, but the big ones are on weekends. You have to meet certain safety requirements. Helmet, seat belts, roll bar. I can fix you up."

In his first race Purcell found himself being caught in bad positions going into the turns and he finished next to last. But the following Saturday he finished fourth.

"You learn fast," the driver of an Austin-Healey told him.

"Sometimes," Purcell replied. "But I get pretty scared out there. More afraid of marking up my car than anything else, I guess."

"How's your insurance? You'd probably feel better if you carried more than just the track minimum."

"You could be right," Purcell said, buffing the roof of his car with a chamois. "You could be right."

Just as he had fallen asleep that night, the telephone

rang. "Where have you been?" Phyllis asked. "I've been calling all day." Purcell turned on the lamp by his bed to check the time. "Stuart is asking about you, Jim. He can have visitors now. He's so changed." Her voice became hoarse. "I don't mean to cry, Jim, but I just can't stay on top of things here. The car hasn't been running right, the oil burner came on in the middle of the hottest day last week and it cost seventy dollars to get it shut off and fixed and the damn dog got sick and I had to have him put to sleep and now the kids won't talk to me, but what could I do? He was wheezing and spitting up blood all over the rugs. I thought he'd swallowed a bone but the vet said he had cancer. Can you imagine?" Purcell turned out the lamp. "Please go to see Stu. Please. He seemed so different to me today."

On Saturday Purcell planned to visit his brother, but when he reached the turn for the prison he suddenly steered the Porsche away and went directly to the track. "I could win today," he thought. "I have a little experience now."

But at the end of the third lap his car left the track, rolled over once and landed back on its wheels. The man with the Austin-Healey was riding on the crash truck. "You were late out of the turn," he said. "You oversteered."

Purcell walked around the car, running his hand over the dented blue roof. "It happened so damn fast," he said.

Phyllis was in the kitchen when he got home. He told her about the accident. "I should think that you'd have had enough of cars for the rest of your life," she said. The front of her dress brushed against his driving jacket. "You smell like a gas station," she said softly. "Grease."

"You smell like a gin bottle."

She slid one hand around his belt and up under the back of his jacket.

"What are you doing here?" Purcell asked. "What do you want?"

"I just want you to be careful. Come on, don't you ever smile? Do you think Mary would want you to be so unhappy? Look at what Stuart did to me and I'm getting over it, aren't I?" Purcell looked down at her, the scent of her body and hair rising against his face. Her hand pulled his shirt loose from his belt and her fingers moved onto the skin above his waist.

The following Saturday Purcell made the turn toward the Federal Prison. At one o'clock the prisoners clattered down a flight of metal steps and into the room where the visitors were waiting. Purcell shook his brother's hand and they sat down on chairs which were fixed to the floor.

"I'm surprised they let us meet like this," James Purcell said. "I thought there would be glass or a screen."

"It's minimum security here," his brother said. "Just cheaters and swindlers. And draft dodgers."

"Why didn't you appeal? You could still be free."

"I did what they said I did. It was no accident. I thought I could get away with it."

"You're a lawyer. You should know better."

"I know the law," his brother answered.

They talked about life in prison and his brother said: "At least when they lock the cells at night you don't wonder why you feel trapped and surrounded by criminals. Many things are clearer here." Then he asked: "Has Phyllis been coming to see you?"

"This has been hard on her, Stu. She . . ."

"She has a key to your front door. I don't know where she got it but she has it and she's been taking Mary's clothes and jewelry. She wore some up here last week and I got the story out of her. I don't suppose you knew that."

James Purcell was silent.

His brother smiled. "Women," he said. "If you ever marry again, Jim, find a woman who can pull her own weight and who loves you with all her heart because there's only one thing worse than a wife who hates you and that's a wife who loves you only a little."

"Do you see that?" someone said.

James Purcell looked up. Down at the end of the room, seated on a straight-backed bench, was a man in the gray prison uniform. He had drawn up one of his legs beneath him, heel on the edge of the bench, thigh leaning inward to partially cover the head of a woman in a green dress whose face was pressed into his lap, one hand cupped about the side of her mouth as her head slowly raised and lowered. The man, his face almost touching her hair, seemed to be talking to her.

"I don't believe it," James Purcell said, getting to his feet. "Where are the guards?"

"Shut up!" his brother said, grabbing him by his jacket and pulling him backwards. "Shut up and sit down."

After Purcell had watched his brother walk back up the stairs he joined the other visitors. They passed through a series of locked doors in single file. Purcell paused to adjust his dark glasses and when he rejoined the line the woman in the green dress was in front of him. In the parking lot she stopped, searching in her bag. Purcell stopped behind her. She looked up. "What are you looking at? What do you want?"

"Please," James Purcell said, stepping towards her. "Please, you see . . ."

The woman backed away, bending a radio aerial beneath her as she slid along the fender of a station wagon. "Stay away from me!"

"No, please . . ."

"Get away, do you hear? You're disgusting!" The aerial sprang back quivering. She ran among the cars.

Purcell had not reached the main road when the rain began. "No races today," he thought. At a stop sign he buckled the seat belt tight across his lap. He knew the rainwater would fill the dents in the roof and rust the unpainted scratches. "I can fix that," he thought.

The Porsche picked up speed, its tires pressing pale streaks on the wet asphalt. Purcell watched the windshield wipers rub away the summer rain. He loosened his collar and reached for the cigarettes in the glove compartment. "There's no reason why I can't learn to drive this car," he said to himself. "There's nothing wrong with me. I'm all right."

8

Harry Mason

Little Siberia

I

Jimmy swiped a snatch of bennies from the hospital. Being greedy I swallowed too many. It took me a while to realize there was nothing on fire. Just my own system singed.

They opened a new place down the road. We won't be getting short timers or young punks anymore. I'll have to fuck my partners or vice versa.

Red says if they ran this hole like the Black Palace Charlie wouldn't of done what he done. Didn't do no good anyway slicing his dick off. Amounted to nothing more than five years in the bug house (cross the mountain) and two lonely balls left even lonelier.

Now Charlie's back in population and Red says the laugh and the stub is on him (Ha Ha).

The Polack is getting to be an old man. I swear I saw him crossing himself last Sunday in the Church of the Good Thief. No matter. He may try to goose God on Sunday but I know he dreams of real asshole all the rest of the week.

What's the outside equivalent?

HARRY MASON, like everyone else, has had his ups and downs. He is currently working as an elevator operator.

I wonder if I'm getting stir crazy. I can no longer do simple arithmetic. Nothing adds up right.

I also imagine I'm a linguist. I make sounds and they make as much sense to me as English—that is—no sense.

Ever since Father Harland died you can't get an uncensored letter out of this joint. The new Priest is an institutional man. Everybody's talking about it—which is odd—considering there's nothing to write and no one to write to.

Smitty the hack had a run in with the P.K. That lazy French canuck cocksucker is gonna have to hustle from now on.

The lid is on—the lid is off—every year it's something new—they can all swing on my joint belladonna—somebody better send me a food package soon or I'm really gonna get mad.

II

It's the Polack, Red and me with the kid trailing about ten paces behind down the dirt hill and Smitty the screw trudging twenty paces up ahead. The kid is trying to catch up to us (feel part of the team) but we walk extra fast so we can map out the plan. Besides we loaded the kid down with the heaviest paint gear—he couldn't catch up if he was Mercury—well maybe Mercury he could but Mercury he ain't, just a skinny raggedy sollypop cow kicker of a kid from Troy or Schenectady or some such hick part. Up ahead we keep an eye on Smitty the hack leading the way, waddlin, oblivious, like some grand dame with his ass-swaying lazy walk. I figure outside of swinging his club over someone's head fourteen times a year, Smitty's only other exercise is fuckin his wife. Probably does that sideways too. Fuck Smitty. The kid too. Double for the Polack and Red! I don't know how come I get into these swindles. I ain't got the time they have. I got more to lose than any of them; if only I wasn't such a sucker for protocol. Yeah, I'm too ethical.

We are about up to the Church of the Good Thief

when the Polack remarks how quiet I am. "Well," I say, "what do you want me to do, sing?"

"No," Red says, "we got the singer behind us."

The Polack laughs.

"I hope you're right," I say.

"I know I'm right," Red says. "Don't you think I know what I'm doing—"

Before I can think of an answer we are already at the church door and apple-cheeked Smitty turns around hustling us into line. He waits till Junior catches up to us all panting with an eager to please smile on his puss.

"Now," Smitty says, "don't know why Jim picked you jokers for this but I understand the whole job shouldn't take more than three hours at the most so I'll be back at twelve and if it's not finished I'll know you boys have been goofin. Is that straight?"

"Sure," Red says.

Me and the Polack and the kid nod, yes sir.

"Okay," Smitty says, "you're on your honor."

"Rather be on his ass," the Polack whispers as Smitty begins his waddling descent down the hill.

"What the fuck are we supposed to paint anyway?" I ask. "I can't even apply mercurochrome evenly."

"Don't worry," Red says, "Jimmy already done the painting. He fixed it all up."

Jimmy is the new Priest's right hand con assistant— he lays out the collars and all (there's a proper way to do even that, he once told me)—and so the whole friggin thing is just a setup so me, Red and the Polack can have a little private interview with the kid.

All of us march into the church. It's really very pretty inside. The cons built it themselves wood plank by wood plank, stone on stone, sort of a tribute to boredom. Cons will do anything to get out of the cell, even build a friggin church.

Jimmy is already waiting for us. Waves us into a side room to the right of the altar.

"This here's the store room," he says, waving proudly

at all the canned goods stacked almost ceiling high against the walls. "And don't take anything: every item is accounted for—I ought to know—I keep the inventory cards on the stuff. I'm only letting you see this room cause it's got a window that looks over the hill—you can spot a hack if one decides to investigate. Here," he says to the kid. "Gimme that." He reaches over to unburden the two heavy paint pails from Junior. "I had to stay up half the night painting Father Murphy's quarters so you guys got nothing to worry about. Just remember to cover me. Keep everything quiet. Well, have fun!" He takes the gear and closes us in the storeroom.

"What's with him?" I ask. "Don't he know we're gonna slap sonny around a bit?"

"Slap who?" the kid says.

"Shutup," the Polack answers.

"Jimmy thinks," Red tells me, "we're gonna fuck the kid with the kid's consent. It cost me six cartons of tailor-mades to rent this room and the bullshit work detail."

"Hey," the kid protests, "who you talkin about?"

"I said shut up before," the Polack says. This time his tone is menacing.

"So what are we going to do?" I ask.

"Don't worry, we'll think of something. Meanwhile why don't you stand yourself against the window and look down the hill."

"You guys are making a mistake." But he don't finish.

The Polack smacks his face so hard that standing there a few feet distance I can see the white fingerprints on the kid's cheeks. Red steps over and lams his balled fist into the kid's stomach knocking him to the ground. Air goes out of him in a whoosh like a busted bag. He sits on the floor panting and looking up at us bleary-eyed.

"You little rat," Red says. "We know you sent a tab to the P.K. Willie got a boat out on account of your tab."

The kid is holding his stomach rocking on the ground.

"Who's Willie?" he manages to gasp out. "I don't know—" Red plants a foot on the kid's head, forces his face to the floor and rolls his head back and forth like a volley-ball.

"Yeah, who's Willie," Red says needling, but the kid still can't get his breath and I walk over to the window and look out and wish I could float through the bars down the hill and up over the wall and rise up like some demented air bubble high and dizzy and part of the wind where human noises and closed rooms don't exist. I look out the window and can think of nothing I'd like to be so much as a simple air bubble. Dimly behind me I can hear the kid getting smacked and the Polack's threatening, "Don't yell, if you make a noise we'll cut your prick off." I hear the muffled sound of body punches, quick breathing and some sort of high whining almost inaudible sound, the kind of whining a bird or owl might hear but not me—us—we're deaf to that sound. After what seems an eternity Red calls for me to come over. I keep telling myself the kid is a rat, remember he's a rat not a kid—a rat!

Red has got the kid's balls naked bent double over and holding onto his own ankles with trembling hands.

"Look at that," Red says. "Nothing but honey could come out of that. You want to go first?"

The kid's body shudders, his legs beneath him actually rock—I wonder how long he can stand that way. "No," I say, "I'll wait. Call me when you're finished." I walk the length of the room back to my escape hatch. I look past the yard—gaze over the walls, see the white painted cottages and the green trees surrounding the prison. Inside the yard it looks like a hobo jungle but outside it might be an advertisement for a model town. I expect to see a woman standing on a porch calling out to some kids or some dog or some guy working on his car. Inside the prison I expect to see someone set up a fire and huddle round it even if it is springtime.

A terrible shriek makes me spin around. The scream seems to go clean through me so that my mouth is open as if it was me that let it go. For a second I can't make out what's happening. I see a white body on all fours like an animal. I see Red spitting in his palms and rubbing it on his cock. He is behind the kid while the Polack is spread out in front of the kid holding the kid's head which is lost somewhere in the Polack's groin. Red reaches in his pocket and lights a cigarette.

"If you yell like that again," he says, "I'll jam this cigarette down your eardrum, do you understand?"

"Don't take your head off," the Polack advises, "just go up and down fast and tickle my nuts with your tongue every once in a while."

I see the kid bob his head frantically. Red and the Polack laugh.

"And if you bite I'll piss down your throat," the Polack adds. The kid's body lurches forward like he's been hit again or like he's like to throw up. But he doesn't do anything. The Polack started grinding his dick in the kid's mouth. Red spits on his cock and I see his balloon buttocks ram forward. The kid's torso jerks up like a mad horse but he doesn't cry out. I turn back to the window.

Everything is quiet behind me now except for heavy breathing and Red's occasionally whispering, "That's how we do with rats—that's how we do—" I can just picture him fucking to this private rhythm, "That's how we do—how we do—how we do—"

I get bored at the window and look at the cans stacked against the wall. I wonder if they are all really accounted for. All those vegetables. All that Spam. All that soup. All the dead sardines. The plucked stringbeans. The lifeless tunas, the peeled tomatoes. "All these things accounted for." It strikes me funny and I begin to laugh. I can't help it—it just strikes a chord and I am staring at the cans and laughing like a maniac. I am laughing so hard tears well up in my eyes. I turn around doubled up with laughing. Red and the Polack have finished with the kid and he's lying on the floor like a dishrag, no like a dehydrated vegetable ready to be canned and accounted for. This thought makes me laugh all the harder.

Red and the Polack exchange glances. They mistake my fit and think I am laughing at them. And I am in a way.

In a way I'm laughing at everything but most of all at something I feel stirring within myself. Finally, I just sit down on the floor and all the humor is gone.

"You sure you're through?" Red asks, wiping his dick on some dirty rag of a handkerchief.

Red and the Polack go out leaving me sitting hard on the concrete floor and the kid lying across the room as quiet as a screw's conscience or my own for that matter. I suddenly realized what brought me up short and why I wasn't laughing any more. Never mind the air bubble bullshit or flapping gracefully through the bars and over the wall, what I really wanted was a piece of the action. Shit I was as hard up as Red or the Polack and if I wanted to I could sneer down at them from my hawk perch but if I wanted to be honest then daddyo getting off the nut mattered more. Even the fact of me sitting listening to the workings of my mind rather than to the kid's stillness was proof of what mattered most to me. Me. That's what. And my prick stood up in my pants as if I needed another witness.

I got up and walked over to where the kid lay. If he was faking it was a good act. I bent down, ran my hand over his buttocks but as soon as I started to find the rosebud with my finger he lurched up and a groan split from his teeth.

"Lay still," I said, "if you do that again I'll put my fist up there and pull out your liver. I know it hurts but it'll be over in a minute. So stay quiet."

The kid stretched out mournfully again and I continued. I felt like a doctor and a philosopher all at once. I tried to do it as painlessly as possible but all the same I knew it really didn't matter. I found the hole, the kid quivered, a wet stickiness made me pull my finger out. The sight of blood turned me off. That fuckin Red had lacerated the kid's asshole. The rosebud was bleeding. Screwed up this end for me. Fuckin Red. Such a nice cunty ass too. I climbed over the kid's body and found myself in the same position the Polack had been earlier. The kid's head rested between my thighs and if he hadn't raised his eyes to look up at me I might have spared adding hypocrisy to my long list. As it was that begging look, those greenhorn eyes—I just had to pretend to be his friend.

"Listen," I said. "I had no idea what this was gonna be or I wouldn't of come along but I'm here and you're here so the least I can give you is some good advice." I put my hand on his head just like his daddy might have done. What spoiled the effect and almost made me sick was feeling his matted sweaty scalp; the steam seemed to be oozing up through his brain. Those shit kicker's eyes started to well up looking first at me and then upwards toward the ceiling. "And don't start sniveling," I said harshly. "Look at me and you're looking at a cold wall. I can't help you and if you look further up you're gonna bunk into a tremendous can of Campbell's soup. All I can tell you is how to take care of yourself so you don't get this deal again. First of all you shouldn't have ratted. As far as the population goes that justifies anything that's been done to you—"

The kid was nodding his head denying he was a rat. I don't think he was able to talk, he just kept nodding the head going no with his eyes saying no all so desperately sincere I almost believed him.

"Anyway it don't matter now whether you did or didn't. The thing is you got to live with us not with the screws so regardless you better not rat on us about this. Red and the Polack are my partners, they're doing thirty to life and got nothing to lose so keep your mouth shut from now on and you'll be all right. All you got is a slight cut on your lip, it's healing already and when you get back to the cell block stick a wad of toilet paper up your behind. And leave it there. That'll clear up too. When you go to the shower Saturday make sure you shower at the far end away from the hacks. You got some body bruises and if you let them see that, that's another way of ratting. Understand: don't let the hacks see the bruises."

The kid was hanging on to my every word like it was the gospel and in a way it was. He was really a sweet little bastard which only made it worse for him. I kept wishing he would be punkish but you could tell this one wasn't. You could just see him going out on a Saturday night passing final inspection from some approving old lady who beamed at his appearance and never doubted that the outside world would treat her boy just fine. Well it was almost enough to make me lose my hard-on. Almost.

"Okay," I said, "enough bullshit. I can't waste too much time. Now look, I know you're not a fag and not a punk and you may not even be a rat and maybe later on we'll become friends but right now you gotta take care of me too. I'm not asking you to enjoy it—like I said I know you're no fag and I'm not even gonna insist that you do a good job, you wouldn't know how. I'm making it as easy as I can for you. So just close your eyes and open your yap and I'll do all the work."

If the kid was disillusioned with me he didn't show it. He didn't show anything. I looked at his tight shut eyes and open mouth and was reminded of a fox terrier I once owned. Good dog too. He'd wait on his hind legs for a full five minutes if I ordered him to—though the older I got the fewer were the orders I gave him but here I was back with my old order-giving nature, no longer fooling myself that I had ever discarded it.

I fucked the kid in the mouth and came off in a minute holding his head down to make sure he swallowed all of it not bothered by his inward heaving and the gagging sound he made as I drained my pipes. Then I buttoned up my fly and went outside to join the others.

Jimmy, Red and the Polack were playing cards seated on the red velvet carpet upon a raised platform with a miserable lookin statue of Christ looking down on the proceedings.

"How's it going?" I said to no one in particular.

"Shit," Jimmy answered. "This fuck just won back two of the tailor made cartons he gave me to hire the church."

"Quit complaining," Red says. "You're still four to the good. Who asked you to call my bluff. I don't bluff."

"How's the kid?" the Polack asked.

"He'll be okay," I said. "You know," turning to Red, "that little stinker still swears he didn't rat on Willie. Listen Red, are you sure you got him dead to rights?"

Red kept looking at his cards.

"I'm trying to figure out my hand," he said.

"Red's always sure of everything," the Polack answered for him.

"Yeah," Jimmy said. "Red never makes a mistake, that's why he's doing thirty too."

"Well, I still like to know."

Red put his cards down in disgust.

"What's the difference?" he said, exasperated. "He was a good piece of ass wasn't he? You had yours didn't you? What's with the fucking interrogation? You want to play police station go bother the kid with your questions."

Everyone got quiet for a second. We looked at each other, we looked at Red, and the Polack almost started to turn sideways to the storeroom but midway he changed his mind and lowered his eyes to his cards. Red picked up his hand again and Jimmy asked him if he wanted more cards or was he staying.

I stared at the plaster Jesus and at a mural directly behind him showing St. Dennis the Good Thief hung on his cross with a couple of soldiers at his feet rolling dice for his coat. I kept staring so intense that I completely forgot where I was and it was a little scarey but for a minute it was like I wasn't looking at all but like I had gone out of myself and was up there. It was the oddest thing.

"What the fuck are you gapin at now?" Red asked.

"Nothin," I said—then "Don't you think it's funny that the kid didn't fight back? I mean didn't even try to?"

"What's funny?" Red answered. "He's a creep kid that's all. The place is overrun with creeps and junkies, spicks and hillbillies and niggers, it ain't like it used to be. There's nobody left anymore—hey where you going—"

I had already stepped off the platform and was making my way toward the storeroom. I seemed to be traveling against my will—the last place I wanted to go was back to the kid but that's where I was headin. My heart was pounding like I was scared or something and the last thing I heard before I opened the storeroom door was the Polack, Red and Jimmy laughing and Red talking loud: "Seconds? Yeah, he's going for seconds. All that bullshit and he's going back for seconds—"

My fingers trembled on the knob, the cold brass felt unnaturally heavy. I took the deepest breath I ever did before entering.

I never got past the instep. My mind reeled and my feet seemed glued to the cement floor. The kid seemed to be sitting up, his knees folded neatly under him while a steady stream of blood trickled from somewhere within him; it rolled in red pencil lines fanning out gradually and soaking the little pile of clothes next to him. His head appeared lopsided snapped back and almost touching his white shoulder. At his feet lay a kitchen spoon, the handle scraped and honed down to razor sharpness. Rays of sunlight filtered through the one window and made a pattern all about him. I counted the light stripes and deep shadows in the room. There seemed to be perhaps three or four separate pools of sunspots and innumerable dark secret places. I kept thinking of me and Red when we were kids and someone in our neighborhood had jumped off a roof. I remembered myself staring and counting the stoop steps while Red beside me told me what he saw. "Jeez look at that. That's his brains there. Looks like tripe or spaghetti smeared with a little red sauce. Jeez, look at that."

And here I was again counting not stoop steps but sunspots and Red behind me yelling. "The little fuck look what he done to us, look what that little fink bastard done to us." And Jimmy, his voice high pitched and panicky. "I had nothing to do with this shit. I ain't getting no bit outta this. I had nothing to do with it." And the Polack muttering, "None of us had anything to do with this. He did it to himself," and Red growling in my ear, "Little motherfucker rat, little motherfucker rat" over and over and over. "Little motherfucker rat" over and over and over. "Little motherfucker rat, little motherfucker rat."

III

Miss Tornicina that liver lipped nigger bitch got put into segregation. Everyone's known for years what a faggot she is but she got busted fucking her old man Jack. What a come down! Jack ain't been out in population since.

Butch split Skippy's scalp with a shovel. Butch is in the box and Skippy is in bad shape up at sick bay but what's really rough is now they won't be permitted to pal out with each other again.

I'm getting tired always walking a straight line. Straight line to the messhall—straight line to the shop—straight line to the showers—never can turn a fuckin corner when I want to—straight line here, straight line there, straight line that place—yeah—if I ever finish up you can bet bugs will crawl out of their shit chute before they get me to walk their straight lines again.

One thing: I'm getting out of the tailor shop and transferring to the rock gang. That's where the action is at. I hear everybody's got their own private hole out there— they dig six feet deep and you can get blowed down there and everything. . . .

Rascha Levinson

Description of a Situation

I was getting more confident every day. It was the way he behaved. For example, when he stayed overnight, it was he who made the breakfast in the morning, not I. Quite a change from the other place.

Of course, I knew there were other sides of his life; he was not involved only with me. He came to see me often, but not every day; I was aware that he had a whole world that had nothing to do with me. He spoke about this world occasionally; sometimes he would talk as if I knew all the people in it, he wouldn't bother to identify them. He would tell me about his plans and projects, thinking aloud, and I would try to be of help. It's difficult to find the appropriate thing to say when you don't fully understand what is being discussed, but I come from a long line of women talented and trained in just this way. Not everyone can say as much.

One day recently we went to a fair in the village; we walked around the grounds, looked at all the booths, and at last stopped in front of the stall where they were selling flowers. He said, "Which would you like to have?" I hesitated, there were so many. There was a silver-leafed plant that I liked, but the woman said it would grow only in a garden. He said grandly, with a wave of his hand,

RASCHA LEVINSON lives with her daughter in Manhattan.

"Take it anyway. If it dies, so much the worse for it." So we took it home and he insisted that it should be put on the dresser in my bedroom, rather than in the living room.

Another time when I invited some people to dinner (which I was allowed to do every so often; otherwise I saw hardly anyone) I sighed that though I was eager for the company, it would be a great deal of work. He indicated that we could have the dinner prepared outside. That had never happened to me before. (To cook large meals for many people was expected. It was part of my job. Not the kind of job where you go out to an office from nine to five, and when you leave there, all of you leaves. No, this job is something I cannot shed, as close to me as my own skin. It has grown to fit me, or have I grown to fit it, I sometimes wonder.) To have him bring food for my guests that some-one else had cooked aroused in me feelings of the most exquisite anguish, as well as some strange sensations which I came later to recognize as joy.

Let me tell you, it was indeed difficult for me to get used to so few people. When I first came I would prepare large meals every evening, as I had been accustomed to do. I would busy myself all day with planning the meal, buying the necessary ingredients and cooking them. There are so many factors to be held in mind: taste, expense, variety, aesthetics; a complicated task. It took me quite a while to realize that most of the time there was no one to eat all the food I prepared. There were days when I could refrain; then again the fit would come over me and I would rush around and prepare a meal for twenty people in one after-noon. When I was able, gradually, to give it up, I felt as if an essential part of myself, an arm for example, had withered away.

I don't know why I keep jumping about in my telling this; it must be that the whole affair, from start to finish, is so puzzling to me. I find it difficult, too, to pin down the various incidents I want to relate; my memory seems to be getting worse every day.

One morning that I remember well he said to me at

breakfast, "But you are so thin this morning. You look even more delicate than usual."

I know I'm not fat; where I came from it had always been spoken of as a fault.

"Look how thin you are!" they would say to me. "Why, just look at your bones, how they stick out! You should eat more, put some flesh on!"

To hear him equate my thinness with delicacy (I knew from my long connection with him how much he and the others of his group prized delicacy) made me realize what an asset it must be in his eyes. The more since he rarely pays me compliments; indeed, I could hardly tell at first why it was that he had, at great cost and trouble, taken me from that other place. In the beginning I had been so puzzled about it that I was silent, and that again worried me; I felt I must be boring him.

I mention these few examples, crude as they may seem to the experienced person, to try to show how our relationship had developed. There were other incidents as well. Some were so slight they hardly bear telling. Or maybe it is that they cannot be put down on paper, consisting as they do of mere gestures, or inflections of the voice, which have no counterpart in words. Perhaps one could make a movie about them.

These incidents I am recounting, I hasten to say, took place over a period of years. You must not imagine that they all occurred together, or in a short space of time—their effects on me would not have been so potent if they had.

There is the ritual of making the coffee. That comes at the end of every meal. As with everything else here, they do it quite differently. In the other place it was brewed in a glass pot and filtered through special papers which removed every trace of oil, while here it is boiled in a metal pot and strained through a fine cloth which insures that all the oils are preserved. I have to say that on the few occasions I have returned to the other place I found their coffee very bad. In the other place there were always complaints about the coffee: it wasn't hot enough, or it was too strong, or too weak. There were mutterings, growls, shouts, and so on. Here it's different. My companion has voiced only pleasure in my conduct of this particular piece of business.

In the other place, as I mentioned before, I always felt at a disadvantage. There was my silence, which is quite natural to me. There they are all great talkers. I remember one girl who would come into the room almost panting to enter a discussion, any discussion. Her eyes popped out of her head, her hands restlessly touched everyone until she found some opportunity to make a remark. People who could talk well were extravagantly admired. Especially those who could argue both sides of the question simultaneously, so that their opponents were not only routed, but superfluous. And those who could turn a witty phrase, or make socially delightful remarks, were highly regarded. Whereas I was always forgetting to say the most elementary things.

I remember once being introduced to a distinguished elderly couple. I knew that the introduction would take place, since they were sitting directly in my path, and I rehearsed quickly in my mind how I would smile and turn from one to the other, shaking hands, and what I would say in the awkward pause that always follows the mentioning of names. I knew if I didn't think about it beforehand I would lose my head, as I usually do, and the whole affair would be a horrible fiasco. When I got to where they were sitting, everything went off as I had foreseen; I said everything properly and shook hands first with one and then with the other. The man got up when he saw there was to be an introduction, and instead of saying, "Oh, please don't get up on my account," or "No, no, do sit down," and smiling graciously, I said nothing at all, and so he was forced to stand there, poor man, until I had gone. And I didn't even realize he had been standing on my account until much later, after I had left them!

The people in the other place didn't say anything to me about it; they didn't need to. I had been there a long time and I knew very well what was proper and of value in their eyes. In those days I took their values to be absolute,

I never knew there were any others (it has taken me a very long time to find that out, I'm afraid) and every time I thought of not saying "Oh, but do please sit down" I had to shake my head to drive the sound of that unspoken phrase out of it.

When I came here it took me quite a while to realize that the silence I possess, the hesitancy and, yes, even the lack of social manner, the ability not to say the right thing, were actually considered to be a mark of superiority. Slowly, in a confused way, I perceived it, and then I became bold enough to recount incidents like the one I have just described to my companion. Instead of receiving my story in a frigid silence, or in didactic fashion ("Next time you should say—"), he said, "Yes, but your eyes are so large." Another time he said, "Let your hair fall over your face." And I saw that he and his associates, the people who came here from time to time, did admire my eyes and my hair. Sometimes, in corners, they told me so. If I could only learn to let them see just how hesitant I am, which is even more than may appear (since I have always made great efforts to hide this same hesitancy), I'm sure it would help me in the situation I am now facing. But I will come to that.

Have I been able to make you understand how, gradually, since I came here, my feelings have changed? Day by day I seem to have grown more delicate but also stronger, and, I can only call it, brighter; I feel at times there is a light inside me.

For instance, in the nocturnal activities which are so large a part of life, my training has been extensive, though nothing was ever said. All the same the training was very rigorous; but in the old style. In spite of certain appearances there was nothing modern about it. So that when I came here, where they are up-to-date in many areas, there was another surprise waiting for me. At first, whether because of my newness or for some other reason I couldn't say, everything remained the same. But gradually on the long nocturnal wanderings, our positions changed and it was I who led and my companion who followed. Not all the time, of course, but we discovered something that had been overlooked in my previous training: I had a talent for negotiating marsh land, I could move easily among the tall grasses; they seemed to bend before me and rise up again after me; they seemed to welcome my coming. I didn't mind walking through the thick milky liquid, as many women do; I quite enjoyed it—I liked the feeling of being bathed in this soothing element. My companion was delighted with my abilities and urged me, after a while, to develop them further. For instance, he would suggest to me various ways of handling the grass, ways of making it rise up, and then again, of making it lie down. At times, each stalk would stand up so stiffly for me, as I made my incantatory gestures along its length! When we returned after prowling about in the moonlight, deliciously exhausted, we fell asleep quite content. Other nights, I seemed to have lost the proper touch and we came back, dissatisfied and worn out. But gradually, over a long period of time, the nights of failure became fewer. Successes were more frequent, and even more pleasurable. I became proud of my abilities, which my companion assured me were far in excess of those of others he had known.

At this point I can't make out whether all the encouragement was given to me to make my present fall (but is it a fall?) harder, or whether what has now occurred is simply a temporary happening. Perhaps it has been ordered by some superior of my companion's (provided he has a superior, which I can only surmise) as a test for me. I am at a loss to explain what has happened, though I puzzle myself with it constantly.

To be brief, what has happened is this: another woman has been brought into the house. She is shorter than I am, a bit older, and by no means thin. She is rather heavy through the neck and shoulders; not fat, but broad. At first glance she is not very prepossessing, but I have learned that people change their faces under the influence of new surroundings, new values; features that were once oppressive can recede into the background and one suddenly sees that, to take a random case, the mouth which had

previously appeared domineering is simply courageous. To a
sensitive eye, forms that are not perfect have their interest.
So I am on my guard, though someone else might wonder
why I am afraid. Especially since the change that has taken
place since she arrived here seems to be all in my favor. I
mean that since she has been here, her body has grown
heavier, though her face has remained the same. It seems to
me that every time I see her she has blown up a little more,
as if she were a balloon. I use the metaphor advisedly: not
only is she getting fatter but larger in every direction. I am
afraid someday she will fill up the kitchen and then how
will we manage? I, on the other hand, seem to be getting
thinner and even more transparent, which should make me
feel more confident. But I don't feel reassured, I feel quite
anxious. If delicacy is admired, why was she brought here,
when to begin with she was gross in appearance? Are there
other qualities that are equally admired here, qualities of
which I have heard no mention until now, qualities which
I lack and this woman possesses?

One evening as we happened to be sitting together,
she told me about an incident which had occurred on her
way here. It was very cold where she came from; she had a
fur coat, everyone there had a fur coat. But when she left
the country, she was obliged to leave her coat. She didn't
want to leave it, she argued, how she argued and fought,
twisting this way and that in her efforts to hold on to her
possession! In the end, valiant though she was, she had to do
as they said. She told this story at great length—she seemed
to be very sad at her loss—but also in a clowning way, acting
out all the parts in the story: the people who were bringing
her here, and those at the customs office where the argument
took place.

The new woman described all this to me as we sat in
the kitchen. Her grossness flickered and became, what? I
asked myself. The domineering quality which was so evident
in her face and body did not disappear, but it receded
somewhat. I found her sympathetic at that moment. We
have not talked again since she told me this story, only

exchanged banalities and those social remarks at which I am so bad (she is much better at them than I, I notice).

Since this woman arrived, my companion has only been here once. As you can imagine, I kept a sharp lookout for anything strange, but everything was as it has been, except for one small incident.

We were sitting at the table in the kitchen, I in my place and my companion in his, with the new person on the other side of him. My companion complimented me on the dinner, which pleased me a great deal. The new woman had managed to make a dish by herself, though I don't know how since I was working in the kitchen all afternoon, and she wasn't in there. It was some little stewed side-dish, a deep red color. It stood next to her plate and she offered my companion a taste of it after he had admiringly commented on the color. I joined him in admiration because it was indeed very beautiful. I expected that he would pass the dish to me so that I could also taste it. But he didn't do that at all; after he took some he passed the dish back to her. As he held the dish out, and she reached out her hand for it, the two collided and the dish was upset, the beautiful crimson liquid spilling on her arm and down the front of her blouse. She started and cried out in distress. My companion was quite upset; he apologized again and again. Taking his napkin, he attempted to wipe the liquid from her blouse. As he brushed her blouse, printed with flowers of pink and red, the same vivid red as the stains, it seemed to me that the air of the room grew tense; I heard a curious sound, the sound of an electric storm one can hear coming from a long way off.

"Oh, it's nothing, don't bother."

"Not at all, I'm so terribly sorry."

And then the incident was over.

I was upset by this occurrence, as you can imagine. I didn't know what to do—whether to say anything to him or not. I was longing to be reassured, but I was afraid that if I did say something, I would only succeed in fixing the incident in his mind and increasing its validity and its dangerous aspect. Whereas if I kept silent, and the incident perhaps did not have the significance I attached to it, all might be as before. After all, I'm not even sure that the new woman is here on a permanent basis.

My companion left the next morning, after spending the night in my bed, as usual, but I remain agitated. He is never able to tell me when he will come back, and this time is no different, but I await his next visit with a trepidation I have not felt since the early days. I have no idea what will happen the next time. Maybe the new person will leave as she came. Maybe she will stay and get fatter. Maybe there is going to be another, a different incident, whose exact form I cannot predict.

And what will happen to me? Maybe I will continue to get thinner and more transparent until I disappear altogether; I don't know.

Bill Amidon

Daddy What Does Dead Mean?

As the generation of leaves, so is that of men.—*Homer*

Jesse Faulcon received a phonecall at Shondors (the Lower
EastSides superbar on Avenue B) one afternoon informing
him that his father didnt have long to live andthat he had-
better get himself backthere quickly if he had any intention
of everseeing the man alive again. He wrote a note to Mitzi
left it at the bar with Dion and didnot even go home:

> *I have to split for awhile. I took*
> *all $100. If you need bread borrow*
> *it from your fucking father. See you*
> *in awhile.*
>
> > *Like,*
> > *Jesse*

He took a bus to The NewJersey State Truckstop and
pickedup a semi to Harrisburg got a secondlift from Harris-

BILL AMIDON is a former gang-kid, record promoter and artist's
model. His contribution is a chapter from his novel, *Charge . . !* ,
published this spring.

burg to Pittsburgh and took a bus from there to Cleveland. It all took him twelvehours and he was at his mothers house by four in the morning.

Jesse's dad hadbeen in the veterans hospital for nearly ayear and Jesse knewthat he was probably getting tired of it. Hospitals are a bore—worse than subways/chicks fathers/or jail and Jesse wouldnt have blamed his father for dying.

He saw him in a room with three otherthings that usedto be men. He was a tender zombie. It was nearly impossible for Jesse to look at him. To be near him. His head was a skull drapedwith skin the color of rosecloth. His eyes were glazed and he kept them partly open when he slept. That was the way he was when Jesse firstwalked into the room thinking that he was too late. His eyes in that condition caused Jesse to remember something someone had said only weeks before in Shondors: if you can see the whites of a persons eyes beneath the pupil it means that that person is about to die. He didntknow what that hadto do with anything but it creeped him.

He pulledup a chair and sat by the bed staring at the bulging stomach under the crispness of sheet. It was grotesquely enormous. As though he—a man—was about to give birth. What monstrous thing—what absolute gargoyle could the first parturient male bring forth? what Gorgon? what triple-headed Stheno-Euryale-Medusa snake-covered pates writhed in his interior hungering for life lusting to turn the world to stone? His navel had disappeared completely and violet scars circumvented the pale blanch of his waning flesh like seams on a tragic basketball. His legs were as skinny brittle and white as uncooked spaghetti. His arms were like long figbars—exactly thatshape and nearly thatcolor splatteredwith purple scabs bruises needlemarks and sores. His hands were the onlything about the man that didntlook dying—but they were unnaturally soft; soft graceful and gentle like the hands of a surgeon or a barber. Jesse's father had always done hard dirtywork and his hands were eternally begrimed and calloused—but then they were soft and it seemedto Jesse had alwaysbeen.

Wyeth Faulcons speech was barely audible generally coming in a hoarse whisper. Almost no one couldhear him and often hadto ask him to repeat something he hadsaid. That made him cranky and short. He felt that everyone around him within earshot was losing his hearing and he said so. He could afford to say that because no one would contradict him. Andso he couldtake comfort in believing it. Whynot? He was dying and mayaswell be rightabout everything forawhile. Dying didhave some benefits. Excepting that he couldnt change his death he could makebelieve whatever he wanted and die happy. Thats why he hopedthat Jesse wouldnt comeback: he knewthat his son would makefun of him for shamelessly playingwith everybodys head. Wyeth couldbe the ornriest sonofabitch on twowheels—and he cried when he was proud. He was sometimes a baby. He would whine and groan and when he did he wanted attention. When he didnt get it he would cuss-out the world. He would ask for sympathy in those obvious ways. When he didnt get it he became sulky and disgusted—more with himself than anyonelse. There were certain aromas Jesse always associated with his father: mansmells he called them: newsprint beer nicotine and an acrid odor of arrested sweat. He remembered him on a Christmas afternoon wearing some sillykindof Wintercap with earflaps pulledown, a can of beer in onehand and an aggressively ugly bathrobe. He remembered running footraces with him from the bustop Wyeth holding his changepocket with onehand and his lunchbucket with the other Jesse everclose enough to see the familiar blackstar on the foggyblack lid of the blackbucket but neverclose enough to catch him or win. They didthat till Jesse was sixteen and his father fiftysix. He remembered poppinghard biceps on skinnyarms thrusting from the loops of his undershirt; he remembered blue and white striped boxershorts and hairless white legs. Wyeth was proud of his son his wholefamily and anylittle accomplishment they mightever have achieved. He had the narrowmind which camefrom driving taxi too long thus was abit of a bigot—and that sorely hurt the man. Deeply. Because he was a sweet sensitive who was gentle and generous. He couldnt understand *why* he believed somethings were wrong and others right when he knewthat it was otherwise . . . but he did and it made him weep more than once. He was loved and liked and he needed to know that—but he was never very respected except by his family. He had neverlived in an atmosphere where anyone respected his peers; he had always lived where people always expected respect for the wrongreasons. Those who couldnot give him respect neverknew why either—but they couldnt—and they didnt. They thought of him as a clown because he was unable not to laugh at himself when he did something dumb or silly. He thought these antics endeared him to others because they were laughing with him—he hadmade them actually laugh! But when his back was turned they shook their heads and felt superior. Wyeth Faulcon needed love from strangers he passed on the street knowing he would never see them again.

The dying man felt a presence in the room and he opened his eyes resuming hatred of the hospital odor ("Goddammit I re*fuse* to get usedto that uglystink!"). He saw his son smiling wearily at him.

"Hey Tough," Jesse said.

His father closed his eyes again and smiled at the ceiling. "Who sentfor you?" he rasped. "Goaway ya bum. Lea me alone."

"Looks like youre gonna die Kid."

"Screw you," his father told him opening his eyes. "Whatsamatter with you? Nobody ever tol you yer not sposta tell people things likethat?"

"Yeah. I was told. Whats it feelike?"

He shrugged. "Shitty. Whattayou *think* it feelslike?"

"I was kinda hopin it wouldbe like a good piece of tail."

"Are *you* in fer a surprise . . ."

"Hurt much?"

"Naahhh. Slike . . . constipation . . . gas . . . headache . . ."

"They giving you anything?"

"Yeah a hardtime."

"Mom says you quit drinking and smoking . . ."

34

"Almost ayear ago ya bum. . . . You should try it. . . . Feelbettern I have in years. . . . I can breathe again. . . ."

"Want me to crankup your bed?"

"Whatfor? Yd only hafta crankit backdown again. . . ."

"Dont startwith that existentialist crap. . . ."

"Whatkinda crap?"

"Nevermind. Mom tells me youve been hallucinating."

"Moms fulla shit. I know what I see."

"Whatdo you see?"

"Birds."

"Birds."

"Yeah birds and dont git smart with me either."

"Whatkindof birds?"

"Whatkinda birds . . . What the hellsa matterwith you? Birdsr birds! How the hell do *I* know whatkind they are? With wings!"

"Dont get your bowels in an uproar. Whatelse?"

"Theres a coloredlady."

"Uh-huh. And what does she do?"

"She does what coloredladies always do." He lifted his arm feebly and pointed to the pipe that ranaround the bed which was attached to the ceiling. "She comes out and sits on thatpipe."

"Out of where?"

"Out of where—outta the *pipe!* Whatsamatter with you?"

"Bullshit. Youre hallucinating."

Wyeth grinned sarcastically. "You knowbetter right?"

"Is she out there now?"

"Dyou see her anywheres?"

"No."

"Then why ask me? You got eyes dontcha?"

"Why do you suppose she's not out now? Does she ever come-out when anyones around?"

"No."

"Why dyou suppose that is?"

"Because I tol her *not* to goddammit!"

"She just sits there huh?"

"Just sits there. Staring at me. Blackbitch makes me nervous."

"Why dont you tell her to goaway?"

"Because I'd rather be nervous than bored."

"She talk to you?"

"Onceinawhile."

"Whats she say?"

"Wouldn you like ta know. . . . Ha-ha-ha . . ."

"You look terrible."

"You dont look so hot yerself. . . . But I'm dyin—whats yer excuse?"

"Living."

"Ya see the kids?"

"Yeah . . ."

"Boy theyre my girls. . . . Beautiful aint they?"

"Yes. Can I get you something?"

"Yeah a diaphragm," he said throwingoff the sheet and revealing the bloatedball of his stomach. "See what yer goddam mother did to me?" Jesse had an emotional speed-ball: he wantedto laugh and cry. He winced. "Look: those goddam sneaky doctors swiped my navel," he said laughing. It hurt. Jesse pulled the sheet backover the ending body.

"Youre gonna make medical history Pop."

"A helluvalotta good its gonna do *me*."

"Gonna leave your body to science?"

"Mightaswell. They got most of it already," he said referring to twothirds of his stomach his appendix yards of intestines a gallbladder his teeth tonsils adenoids foreskin and his recently purloined navel. "On secondthought I think I'll keep what I got and let it rot. The hellwith those bastards. You see your boy?"

"Nope. I dont think his mother wouldlike that."

"Kick er ass—he's your kid too. . . ."

"Thats not the way the law sees it."

"The law sucks. Go see im if you want."

"Maybe I'll just do that Dad."

"I'd kinda like to see him once before I kick. . . ."

"Whatfor? He wouldnt remember you and youd only scare him."

"Yeah . . . I guess so. Whatre you gonna do with yerself Jesse?"

"Wait it out I guess. Try not to get caught like you did."

"Dont kid yerself Jess—I had it alright. Yer mothers a damngood woman."

"I knowthat."

"Bettern *I* ever deserved. An you kids always didright by me."

"I know Dad. I guess . . . I dontknow . . . We'll see . . ."

"Its yer bat an ball. . . ."

"You scared Dad?"

"Nope."

"Really?"

"I ever lie to you? Whats there to be scared of? When you been sick and crappedaround asmuch as I been it dont look so bad."

"I guess not. Look . . . I'm gonna split now. . . ."

"You gonna be intown long?"

"No. I'm leaving now."

"Oh."

"Too depressing."

"I know. Look—when it happens you dont hafta comeback here."

"I know that. I dont hafta do anything."

"Youknow what I mean."

"Yeah. You let me decide about that."

"Its too expensive. I know you aint got any money. I'm sorry I didnt have nothin to leave you kids."

"Youre leaving me morethan youll everknow about. Thanks."

"Youre a goodman Jesse. I love you."

"I love you too Dad." And Jesse kissed him.

As he was leaving the room he turnedto wave at his father and saw him raise his hand slightly from the bed and they both had tears. He knewthat he wouldnever see his father again and that hurt Jesse.

-: * :-

He said goodbye to his mother and sisters and started hitting all the old Saint Clair bars where the steelworkers drank. He worked his way around to all the old Ukrainian and Polish bars where the stench in the mensrooms was nearly unbearable; where men hadto have a boilermaker (shot of whisky in glass of beer) or a depthcharge (drop wholeglass in) before going to work in the morning or home to oldwoman atnight; where useless grampas sataround allday drinking Slovenian highballs (shot of wine in beer) talkingabout oldcountry and how rotten and fulla skatah America is then later fistfighting with some smartass college-kid who thought the country needed changing.

Jesse got thoroughly plastered lushing his way out Euclid Avenue to the University area drinking then with collegekids who all thought he was a verycolorful character and wantedto know more about him and what he thought-about things—afterall "a Bowery Bum may have a more important comment to make about life than a college professor. . . ." He told them Jesse did—he told them 1) suicide is the only answer to the metaphysical problems of the twentieth century; 2) homosexuality purged the psyche of traumatizing experiences; 3) Ozzie Cadena lives; 4) opium is the religion of the minority; 5) *"Rhoda Kittylitter Has Nice Legs";* and 6) honking salt would give you a groovy high. Then he went to sleep at the home of a young blackwoman he had once been abit in love with. He met her husband for the firstime and they dug eachother somuch it was embarrassing.

The nextmorning he said goodbye and went to visit the birthplace of A.E. Kugelmanns fatherconfessor. He got-drunk there on wine and went South to such exotic places as Akron Youngstown Columbus Mansfield and alot of littletowns that made him sick. Silly towns. Adolescent towns. Senile towns. Towns filledwith accordions and petunias. Towns that served Negroes. Barbecued. Towns that thought Jesse Faulcon was just as nuts and useless as he thought the towns were. Uncontested divorce. Onenight twoweeks after seeing his father he sat in a tavern in Erie Pennsylvania and he reached into his pocket to payfor a beer and realized the bill (a five) was his last andthat it was aboutime to be headingback to NewYork.

As he drank thatbeer he consideredthat he found drinking alone had always appealedto him as being romantic; sitting at home with a bottle and a glass as he did the night of Camilla (his bestfriends lovely sister) and othernights around thatime; sitting in a strange bar in a strange town with no one to talk to. He hadnever done much lonesome drinking until that pastmonth and the romance was wearing-off. He was ready to go back.

Dinahmae. That cunt. She had hurt him badly and he was not recuperating. And he thoughtabout Benny poor Benny who walked-off his tenement roof and mangled himself. And his father. And his son who wouldbe nearly what . . ? Seven? Eight? Seven. He wished that he was sitting in Shondors instead of where he was. He feltlike a farmer with a truckload of ready-to-rot peaches. His innocence. His marriage. His son. Girlady. Dinahmae. That cunt. His father. No he was ready to go back. He nolonger *had*to be alone. He'd regained free choice. Something had gone out of him; something had died; something precious hadgone away. Had he missed it it wouldnot havebeen so dear. He didnt even feel it go.

Jesse asked the bartender if there was anywhere he couldsleep thatnight and since Jesse hadspent quite abit in his bar the man said that he couldsleep in his car. He drove Jesse to his house and Jesse thanked him and told him Goodbye because he wantedto get an earlystart on the rest of his life the nextmorning.

Alan Kapelner

The World of Walkers and Runners

As Stan drove up and down the street, he fingered his gun.
And as Stan drove up and drove down the street and fingered his gun, he watched the crowds walk up and walk
down the street. All that walking, and he eyed the walking
legs: the long ones, the short ones, the thick ones, the thin
ones, the regular ones. Stan goddamned the sight. He shot
across Dundee Square. He reached the town's end.

On Highway 31 he quit fingering his gun to scratch
a neck itch. He forgot the itch when he saw Bill Crane's
boy Dave race dogs through fields. He tried hard not to
watch the racing legs, and in the distance was Queen Peg's
Road slicing the highway. He came to it. He steered to get
on it. He again fingered his gun while cruising along it.

He passed Jack Zevrey's farm. He passed three walking girls he didn't know. He passed Jack Zevrey's swimming
hole. He remembered diving into that hole. He remembered
it as he always remembered it when passing it. He remembered how he would dive into it from an apple tree. He
would climb the tree, pick an apple, jam it into his mouth
and dive and rise from the hole with the apple chewed
clean down to the core. He remembered the awe and ap-

ALAN KAPELNER is the author of two novels, *Lonely Boy Blues*
and *All the Naked Heroes,* with a third one on the way.

plause the stunt would get from friends. Those were the days, all right.

He reached Queen Peg's Road's dead end. He slowed the car to a crawl. He squeezed it through walls of trees and over a leafy path that curved into a hushed autumn meadow. He stopped the car. In the background was Holy Top Mountain. In mid-meadow were giant oaks storms had broken. Before him were bushes. Caught on a twig was a napkin he had thrown away the other day. A peach he had disliked was on a chunk of dirt. His car tire imprints of many past visits had flattened the grass around him, and in the intimacy of the meadow, Stan reached into a toolbox. He withdrew stones.

He then gripped his gun. He then leveled it across the car's open window. He then stretched his arm and flung a stone into a tree and the crash of it brought sparrows crying and flying from nests, and Stan sucked his lips, aimed, clicked the trigger and a shrieking bullet killed a sparrow, and in a hunger for more kills Stan flung another stone into another tree and the crash of it brought no life, and he again flung a stone into the tree and again the crash brought no life, and he punched his steering wheel and spit at the dashboard and flung two stones into a bush and two into a tree and one along the grass and two down a path, and as he tensed and gripped and leveled the gun, he heard the brisk sounds of birds and small animals, and a heat fevered him when he saw what he wanted, and two shrieking bullets killed a frightened running rabbit and crow.

Contentment comforted Stan. He sagged in his seat. He petted his gun. He then set it very tenderly across his lap. He then inserted a finger into the gun's mouth and cherished the warmth. He then withdrew from his topcoat pocket a ham and swiss on roll, and he wolfed it.

After a most meticulous napkining of his mouth and brushing of crumbs off his coat, Stan again gripped and leveled his gun across the car's window, and he again flung a stone into a tree and one more followed it. The repetition of the crash brought nothing but irritation from his lips, and he flung another stone and another and three more and one more and the last five along the grass, and no life appeared, and he profaned the animals and the birds for their absence and slammed and fisted the gun's neck and snatched a cigaret from a pack and searched for matches and profaned himself for their absence and roared the car's motor and left the meadow and those he had killed.

The path to Queen Peg's Road was over and done with. Stan passed Jack Zevrey's swimming hole and farm, and he saw and yearned to kill Jack's cat on a run around a pole. He reached Highway 31. He trailed trucks into town. He turned left at Dundee Square, and as he watched the crowds walk up and walk down the street, he fingered his gun.

"Stan, boy!"

Stan hid the gun under a blanket. He watched grinning Charley Casper in a Ford pull up to him and roll alongside of him.

"Stan, boy. Gladda see you."

"Same here, Charley."

"How's it going, Stan?"

"Fine. Never better."

"Gladda hear it. Just saw Wally Angus. Wally's gonna run for Mayor."

"Who isn't, Charley?"

"Wally said he saw you yesterday, and the day before that."

"Where did Wally see me?"

"On Queen Peg's Road, driving past Jack Zevrey's place."

"I haven't been on Queen Peg's Road for months. Wally never saw me, Charley."

"He said it was you. He was with Jack."

"Wally better get his eyes examined before running for Mayor. I was home all day yesterday, and the day before that."

"Whatever you say goes, Stan. Hear from your Ma and Dad?"

"Twice a week. Sometimes three."

"Whatta they say?"

"They keep asking me to come live with them."

"Whatta you say, Stan?"

"No, all the time."

"California's great for living, Stan."

"Not for me, Charley."

"Well, gotta go. Gotta pick up the Mrs. at the five and dime."

"Better hurry, Charley."

Stan turned right. He watched four boys race to a movie, and he skidded over puddles of oil and stopped before an apartment house. He locked the motor. He bundled the blanket around the gun. He then hid the bundle under his coat. His eyes then pained and his face sickened as he reached for and gripped a pair of crutches.

Wriggling his body in a struggle to move from his seat, Stan clutched the car's door. He yanked it open. He jerked his body. He shifted it. He focused it. He plunged it forward at the seat's edge and crutched his lifeless legs out of the car, and he staggered at the curb and fought for balance as Perry Stengel sprinted past him to catch a bus, and he cursed the sprinting legs and cursed his crutching his way to his house. He panted in the doorway. He saw Mr. Graw on a run in the hallway.

"Why the rush, Mr. Graw?"

"Must get those records I was telling you about. You feeling all right, Stan?"

"I'm feeling all right."

"You been out riding again?"

"Again, Mr. Graw."

"You do it every day, don't you, Stan?"

"Every day, Mr. Graw."

"In God's name, where do you go, what do you see? Stan, what do you do?"

"I go nowhere. I see nothing. I do nothing."

"But every day, Stan. You're never home. I rang your bell today, and yesterday, and the day before that, and lots of days before that. Never home. Stan, what are you out for? Why do you take all those rides?"

"What else have I got to do?"

"I don't know, Stan."

"Well?"

"Must go with you some day. Must see where you go and exactly what you do on all those every day rides."

"Anytime, Mr. Graw."

"Must get going for those records. Party's tomorrow. People love to dance at parties. You still don't want to come?"

"Mr. Graw, I told you no too many times."

"Don't understand you young men that live alone."

"Nobody does, Mr. Graw."

"Too bad your folks left you for that San Francisco business."

"They didn't leave me. I made them go. I made them grab the good deal. I said I'd follow later on."

"Will you?"

"No."

"Good God, you lied to your folks."

"Mr. Graw, people not wanting to be burdens are obliged to lie."

"Be seeing you, Stan."

Plates crashing in someone's apartment switched Stan's eyes from Mr. Graw's striding legs, and he maneuvered his legs to his apartment. Keying the lock and opening the door and shutting it was a job. So was the crossing of rugs, and he stumbled over one and fell and rose and tripped over a stool and dodged a desk and lamp and lunged past a bed and flung his crutches to the floor as he flopped into a chair by a window.

Aches jabbed his arms. Sweat pasted his neck. He unbuttoned his coat. He removed the bundle. He unfolded the blanket. He removed the gun. He drummed the trigger. He eyed the street. He saw Alex Taft jump out of a jeep and run over a lawn to call on Ruth Ives, and the jumping and the running gloomed him. He turned from the window. He turned on the radio. He turned it off. He turned on TV. He turned it off. He lit a cigaret. He crushed it. He turned on TV. He turned it off. He lit a cigaret. He stared at a shelf's paper, and that paper, that Cleveland paper, that taking that train for that job on that paper, and all of a sudden, and it was only twenty more small minutes to Cleveland, wheels and whistles and brakes screamed and the train jumped the tracks and plunged screaming people into seas of stone, and he awoke in a hospital's bed and was told his legs were dead.

Stan stared at his crutches. He considered his time. He considered his year of hours spent as a watcher of legs. Wherever he went, by car, by crutch, he would watch legs, walking legs, running legs, countless life-filled legs, and his were dead among them, and they diminished him, second-rated him, drove him to loathe them, war on them, shoot them, destroy them in raging bullet-shrieking dreams that ended in cries to ease realities, and he found a war. It was declared the day he killed a deer.

He was in his car in the meadow. He had brought his gun to test its range when he saw the deer running through the grass. A need to kill the legs that ran was big. He fired one shot. The deer died. That was exactly two months after the death of his legs, and the running deer was his first kill.

Then came five woodchucks. No, it was six. No, it was five. He killed four foxes. That was definite, and the sparrow and rabbit and crow he had killed an hour ago in the meadow followed all the many sparrows and rabbits and crows he had killed all the many hours ago in the meadow, and now in his room the killing of the animals and the birds cheapened him, the deaths degraded him.

He craved ease. He turned on the radio. He turned off a hymn to canned spaghetti. He turned on TV. He saw a comic about to open his mouth. He turned TV off. He turned to the window. He saw a child skip rope. He watched the jumping legs. He watched the rope whiz under the legs' force, the legs' speed, the confident rhythm, the dazzling perpetual motion.

He shut his eyes to shut the sight. He then opened them. He then shut them. He then slowly opened them, and his watching of the jumping legs boiled a hate of the life in them, and a fever stuffed his body, heated his breath, buzzed his ears, wet his eyes, and the sight of his legs dangling and the child's legs jumping swelled the fever, and it pumped him, swelled him, and he rocked and cried the fever and yanked open the window and snatched his gun and leveled it across the sill and aimed at the jumping legs and pulled the trigger and the bullet that shrieked missed the child and shocked the street, and pulsing and oozing like one being drained, Stan saw people fling open windows, lock windows, run into homes, run out of homes, and dogs barked and cars screeched to stops, and Stan watched the child's legs race away in fright.

He then watched crowds pack the street and question the bullet's source. He watched their emotional moving legs. He contemplated his legs. They sickened him. So did his nerves that failed to make his war in dreams a fact. So did his marksmanship that was only good for animals and birds. So did his time on crutches, and he gripped the gun and pulled and pulled the trigger, and as the shrieking bullets shattered, mangled, mutilated the crutches, he heard the crowds roar their finding, and he watched their legs walk and run toward his window.

Stan fisted the gun's barrel. He twisted his body. He jerked it off the chair. He fell to the floor. He crawled on his hands and knees over the shredded crutches. He stopped before his bed. He clutched its post. He yanked his body up and above the bed and dropped into it and bounced on it and sank into it. He then sat up in it. He gripped the gun. He waited for the walking, running legs.

Janet Gerard Chalmers

Tourist Notes

ONE AUTUMN DAY, AT NOON

Something crashed to the ground outside in the back courtyard. We heard the thud and the clang of metal. Then it was quiet.

We waited, as if some explanation would follow, but there was no further sound, except for the steady grinding noise of a garbage truck below in the street, so deceptively reassuring in its ordinariness.

Norah started at the noise. "What was that?"

"It's nothing," I answered, but that familiar feeling of being in the eye of a storm, isolated but safe while others suffer, passed through me like a shudder.

We never heard the sirens. The police, the ambulance came and we were somehow insulated from them by our height, and, even more so, by the intensity of our conversation, our involvement with the children. The phone didn't ring until much later.

I listened as the voice identified itself. A reporter. She began by saying she wanted some information, but as she spoke my mind began extending itself in several direc-

JANET GERALD CHALMERS has received the Elizabeth Janeway Award for Creative Writing. She is the mother of two children.

tions like a growing thing. But stronger than all other feelings was the horror, so that while my answers were polite and perfunctory, I had to struggle to keep my breathing even and my hands from trembling, and when I had put down the receiver and turned to tell Norah, I was barely able to get to the bathroom before my bowels started emptying themselves as they do only in airports, waiting to board a plane.

It was the doorman who finally told me. The body had fallen just a few feet outside the basement window where he was having his lunch. Could he possibly have finished his lunch anyway? Poor Peter. Always ready with a bit of news—the mail is late, it looks like rain, today a girl jumped out the window of the stair landing on the eleventh floor. He is anxious to talk about it. Somehow she got by the relief man. No one knew until two boys came looking for her, asking if anyone had seen a girl run in from across the street in the park. She told them she was going to kill herself. He shakes his head in disbelief. If only she had hesitated they would have found her. Bounced right off the tin roofing of the shed over the garbage, she did.

Only after Norah had left, when the children were napping, did I realize that she must have jumped from the landing outside the service door in the kitchen where I had been cooking. "If you need anything else for the baby you'll tell me, won't you? . . . What?" "Just a napkin, please." "Oh, they're right behind you on the left." "I thought I'd make grilled cheese sandwiches for us, O.K.? I always think of you when we have rye bread." "I see you get the same brand we do."

I went out on the landing, slipping the lock on the door behind me so it couldn't close, my heart pounding, denying reality—unreasonably it seemed that if the door clicked shut the only exit would be the window open before me. I was surprised to find two bars on it—would I even fit? Had she stopped to wonder? After racing past the doorman up eleven flights of steps, are you so filled with adrenalin that you are capable of just plunging out the first open window you see, filled with purpose, sure of success?

I looked around for some sign that she had been there. Some smudge, something dropped, but the grey metal emptiness of the staircase revealed only a cigarette butt stamped out, surely the careless discard of some policeman, knowledgeable in such situations, sure of himself as he never would be were she alive, saying, "This is where she did it."

Or did she wait, standing there a moment to catch her breath, listening to me call to Norah of bread and things, hoping small hopes that I would open the door and find her, that the boys she had talked to would come, that the doorman would catch up? Did she wait until I had finished and gone back into the dining room, wait until it was quiet once again, her aloneness crowding her toward a decision? Had she tried to get through the bars, carefully lifting her leg over, not sure she would fit, then her body, passing through the narrow space, her feet on the ledge outside, hands still holding the bar, then shifting her hands to the lower bar, her feet dangling, until there was nothing left but to let go, no way back, no one to say stop, just a long rush down, deep into the courtyard, crashing on to the tin roofing that protects the garbage?

There was a note in the newspapers, but only name, address and facts of death—not the society girl the reporters had hoped for, just a girl from the Bronx. If she had dashed out of any other park than Washington Square, into any other house than one next to the park, it wouldn't even have been reported. But everybody wants to know about a hippie —even if she's just from the Bronx.

I might have opened that door—to put out the garbage or an empty milk bottle. If the apartment had not been so filled with life, with the noise and confusion of the daily routine, the sharing of food, I might have heard her. Would I have shared with her, opened my world to her. For I know I am afraid of the stranger at the door.

A girl, standing out alone in the park, just the day before. Dungarees, her mother's angel, long curly hair golden, a halo so bright in the sun I could hardly see her face, just the hair and her hand held out. "Can you give me some money, I'm so hungry." The hippie come-on, both real and void of reality, always a test of both giver and receiver. I passed her with a slight shake of my head to indicate no and watched, peripherally, as she walked over to a waiting young man and took a puff of his cigarette, but I felt only the smallest relief from the sadness that engulfed me.

And finally, a week later in the elevator . . . "The doctor said she broke every bone in her body. It was a woman doctor from the police department, you know."

How horrible, I think, and at the same time hear myself saying it, though I am really wondering if she was conscious as she fell. I step out of the elevator and search out my key from my pocket with one hand, the elevator man still standing there without closing the doors, shaking his head, disapproving, his words, "God should have punished her and let her live to be a cripple. She had everything to live for, good health, youth."

His cruelty stuns me. I answer, not wanting to, perhaps from habit. "But maybe no one loved her."

"How did she know someone wouldn't have loved her tomorrow?"

I hunch my shoulders to shut him out, putting the key in the apartment door. He slides the elevator gate closed, his whole day a series of unfinished conversations, my silence has no significance. I enter, allowing the door to slam shut behind me. How many tomorrows can you wait for? Every day part of me jumps, plummeting to the ground.

Today they are repairing the tin roofing that protects the garbage in the courtyard. It seems there is enough money in the building's budget for repairing the damage caused by a falling body. It seems there is always money to pick up the pieces and reestablish the order.

WAITING

I have been waiting ten minutes already, long enough to wonder if it isn't the wrong night, if there hasn't been a change in the address. I evaluate each passerby as a wouldbe door-opener, or comrade-in-waiting, or attacker, though I am unwilling to admit even to myself that I am afraid.

A heavy woman in black, ageless and anonymous, comes out of a building down the street and, after walking by and looking me over, stops to ask if I know a nice girl who might want to rent a room from her. Someone who doesn't take dope and things like that. I am vaguely flattered and amused to be mistaken for a nice girl after such a long time and try to discourage her gently, fighting down the temptation to say something that would shock her.

We say goodnight and she goes back into her building and I am alone again in the darkness, lulled by the sound of the cars passing on the avenue. I watch calmly as a large figure, silhouetted against the street lights, comes from across the street. A young man, whistling. Something classical. Something from college. Bartok, Concerto for Orchestra. Alex could whistle it straight through. I can almost hear it as it should be, the hi-fi blaring, bass turned up, filling you with the sound of the organ. I cannot believe that a mugger would whistle Bartok, not even in the East Village. He passes in front of me, disinterested and not the least bit threatening, and tries the door. But he is no more successful than I have been earlier.

I am encouraged enough by his arrival to say, somewhat awkwardly, that I have been waiting a long time already, but his response is abrupt—someone will be here soon. It is the only information he will offer. I don't even know if he means the same someones I do. And I find that his arrival has been only the smallest consolation. I am engulfed by a sense of isolation more severe than when I had been alone.

At least now it is just a matter of time. I am no longer on my guard, only a little tired and annoyed at myself for coming so early and putting myself in this position. I hardly notice, and then only with impatience, when a black man, an unlit cigarette in his hand, his hi-there, how-do-you-do, go-screw to white middle-class America, comes lurching and unpredictable around the corner. I watch to see how this tall stranger leaning next to me against the building, so silent and uncommunicative, will handle the situation. I note how he moves away from the doorway and further out into the middle of the sidewalk as the Negro comes closer and it becomes obvious he will be approached. He moves without taking my presence into account, but I follow his example, standing to one side of them.

And he handles it well, not just cool, but involved. He takes on the problem of the unlit cigarette as you would the untied shoe laces of a small child, with understanding and just the right amount of concern. He makes an effort to find a match, but does not have one. I am relieved when they part amicably and only notice later, with some embarrassment, that the unlit cigarette, revealed in the street light as the black man passes, is merely a butt, his threatening figure the stooped pathetic posture of an alcoholic wrapped in a coat several sizes too large for him. I move back to the shelter of the doorway and barely notice as he reaches the corner and crosses the street.

I feel more trusting of my companion now, having seen his kindness, even if it has not been intended for me. He whistles again. Now the theme from *Orpheo Negro*. I try to close myself off from it, but its notes, full of all the joy and sadness of Brazil, waken my memories and emotions. I try to escape by walking down to the corner, resentful that a stranger could so quickly reach my very core. He might have reached out and touched my breast as impersonally as he had tried the doorknob. My eyes fill with tears of frustration and loneliness, unable to share or even express my thoughts to him—for what would they mean after all?

And part of me watches the elongation of the street lights viewed through my water-filled eyes, a part of me I must save, untouched. For someone will come with a key for that door and I will have to play it cool. That's what they always want.

David Nemec

Sleep of Soldiers

Recruit Manders was stunned by the rumor. It had the effect of a rifle shot fired past his ear. In shocked silence he sat in the bleachers at the Fort Knox Atomic Reaction Range, a searing ache moving in behind his eyes. On the scarred wood platform in front of the bleachers an instructor from Regiment was describing the exercise for the afternoon. Manders saw but did not hear. He was experiencing an acute dissolution.

The way the rumor went his entire company would be in Vietnam by Christmas.

In a more conventional setting Manders would not have taken the rumor seriously. Although the situation in Vietnam was growing more precarious every day, danger did not yet seem imminent, particularly not the kind of danger that would involve a rudely disciplined unit still in Basic.

But Manders had quickly learned there were few conventions in the Army. From his first morning in the Reception Center—when a Mexican corporal had routed him out of his bunk, screaming, "Off your meat and on your

DAVID NEMEC, former teacher and parole officer, has published stories in *The Transatlantic Review, Works,* and elsewhere.

feet, Oriental cannon fodder!"—rumors had spread around him like wildfire, and many of those rumors, which at first hearing seemed incredible, turned out to be true. After the speed march to the trainfire range, during which a full platoon of men had fallen nearly unconscious from heat exhaustion, Manders could no longer doubt the story that his company was known disparagingly throughout the Post as Double-time Charlie. Then there was the rumor about no passes during Basic, which was confirmed with dreadful certainty when McGurrin, whose wife was having a difficult childbirth in a hospital barely twenty miles from the Post, was refused permission to go to her and only learned by belated telegram that his son was stillborn.

For one week and then another, as the training cycle wore on and the cold rains of late Kentucky autumn began, Manders had struggled through phase after phase of his Basic, tramped for miles through oozing wet mud, up Misery Hill, down Agony Hill, crawled the abrasive sand of the infiltration course, washed the Company Commander's Doberman with a toothbrush, and lived from one moment to the next in wonder of what new torment the following day would bring.

He was not alone in his dissolution, of course. Early in the cycle all the recruits in the company had lost confidence in their cadremen, and as one anxiety heaped upon another, they had begun to lose confidence in themselves. Where in the beginning they had been angered by even the most insignificant rumors, such as the one about saltpeter in their potatoes, they were now oblivious to everything. Whatever spirit of rebellion they had known was blunted by the dreary, almost patternless, existence of Army life. There was a meaning to it, perhaps, but it was obscure; there was an end to it, perhaps, but it was remote. To many of the men, yanked for no apparent reason from jobs and graduate schools and young wives, the rumor about Vietnam came almost as a relief. However horrifying, it brought their long weeks of training sharply into focus. Christmas in Vietnam, an unpleasant prospect to be sure—but in an absurd way here at last was something they could count on and look ahead to.

Manders, however, had not yet reached the point where he could look upon the rumor with any such detachment. Coming as it did after so many weeks of confinement, it was the last straw for him. Where before he had been able to examine even the most devious stories that were filtered down to him with some objectivity, now he had lost all power to react. He could neither accept nor reject the rumor about Vietnam; on one level of his consciousness it registered indelibly, but on the level above it left no impression at all.

In a state of almost complete automatism he climbed down from the bleachers and followed the other recruits in his company to the line of foxholes that faced the Atomic Reaction Range. The exercise was a simple one, no less meaningful than a dozen similar exercises the company had performed in the past weeks. Under frontline battle conditions the men were positioned two to a foxhole, and each man was issued an eight-round clip of blank ammunition which he was to fire off on signal at a dilapidated shack in the middle of the range. Afterward a simulated atomic explosion was to be set off, while the men in each foxhole, working as a team, secured themselves against the explosion beneath their ponchos.

As the range sergeant gave last minute instructions, Manders' mind was filled with thoughts of Christmas alone, dug in a muddy field—and before he knew it, the range sergeant had finished and all the other men had been paired off, leaving only Ogden, the seventeen-year-old recruit from Arkansas, as his partner for the exercise.

Working with Ogden was something of a risk. There was a vast carelessness about him that made him easily the most avoided man in the company. Scarcely two weeks before, on the hand grenade range, he had tried to pull the pin of his grenade with his teeth and had ended up dropping it fully primed at his feet. Only the alertness of the range safety officer, who had scooped up the live grenade and hurled it down range where it exploded harmlessly in the charred undergrowth, saved a brutal disaster. The marvel was that Ogden had come so far in Basic without killing someone or being killed himself. Even the simplest task became hopelessly muddled when he undertook it. In an attempt to make lemonade he had stuffed chunks of a lemon stolen from the mess hall into his canteen. There they had remained for so long, floating on the surface of the tepid water, that they rotted. Ogden, however, had continued to drink from the canteen until the mixture became so foul it made his mouth smell like a straddle trench.

Manders took his place in the last foxhole on line and did his best to ignore Ogden. Lost in the caving of his own thoughts, he leaned against the rain-sodden sand bags that banked the foxhole and stared off across the fogswept land. Although the air was still for the moment, rain clouds were rolling in rapidly overhead, and it was apparent another storm was building. Drawing on a cigarette, which he concealed under his poncho, Manders could almost imagine he was in a foxhole on the perimeter of a remote rice field and the shack in the distance was the outpost of a band of Viet Cong guerrillas. It was a disconcerting vision, and he tried to push it aside. Before he could do so, however, Ogden intruded on him, slamming the bolt of his rifle, furiously impatient to begin the exercise.

"Cool it," Manders said. "Just cool it, will you."

Ogden looked up, his helmet pulled low over his pale eyes. "Cool what?"

"Everything. Quit making a production out of it. . . ." Manders stopped, aware suddenly that he had reached a moment where he could no longer ignore Ogden, just as he could no longer turn away from the natural direction of his thoughts. Ever since his induction into the Army his sense of the present had been diminished, confined to a single training company cut off from the rest of the world, with time no longer a consideration, the days long and vague and hypnotic, inseparable from the weeks. But the rumor about Vietnam had destroyed all that. It had cut through to remind him that the Army was not simply another of those dull and meaningless assignments that were an unavoidable part of life. The Army could, when the occasion arose, assume a purposeful, if inscrutable, design; and that realization made everything suddenly intolerable. It made the whole thought of war vivid to him, immediate and near at hand. It did the worst thing that could have befallen him; it made him wonder who he was and what it would mean to die.

There was no way to avoid it. Even as he rejected it, he knew there was nothing really to reject. His destiny; war; his heritage. Just as there had been an Argonne Forest for his grandfather, and an Iwo Jima for his father, and a Korea for his brother, there was a Vietnam for him. It had been there all the time, waiting for him, inevitable, inescapable.

Ogden was absorbed in other concerns. "Think if I asked, they'd let me have another clip of ammo?" he said.

"What for?"

"I dunno. I'd just like to have one."

"You really dig this stuff, don't you?"

"What stuff?"

"These exercises. This training."

"Beats thinkin about Nam, don't it?" Ogden said. "What's to think about? If we go, we go." He seemed almost cheerful.

What's to think about, Manders repeated to himself. Christ! He drew savagely on his cigarette. It had begun to rain, and with the rain came a cold wind that whipped the low-hanging branches over the foxhole like steel blades. He threw his poncho over him and closed his eyes, trying to doze.

He was shaken out of his ease by a command from the range sergeant to load all weapons. Gleefully, Ogden shoved his clip of blanks into his rifle and snapped the butt plate into the pocket of his shoulder. At much greater length Manders loaded his own rifle and slid into position against the forward flange of the foxhole. Both of them stared down range at the shack, which was visible now only at those rare moments when the wind lifted the curtain of fog. The rain had begun to fall harder and they squinted into it, narrowing their eyes to slits, as if at any instant an enemy platoon might come over the rise.

With the rain pelting their ponchos and the force of the wind behind them, they waited for the signal to commence firing. And waited. What now, Manders thought, why always this waiting?

Ogden shouted into the wet mist, "This here's like real combat, fella."

Manders nodded morosely. Indeed, with the rain dripping down his neck, with the slippery rusted rifle in his hands, and every muscle in his body throbbing from all the damp and sleepless bivouac nights on the cold ground, he had the weird sensation that somehow he had been transported across time and distance to a desolate and godforsaken battlefield. This is the way it really is, he thought. A cold shudder passed over him. Combat. Old newsreels of rotting corpses being carried in tattered litters flashed through his mind . . . the Bill Mauldin cartoons of the trenches and the mud . . . always the mud. . . .

When at last the signal came down the line to commence firing, there were shouts of disgust from every foxhole. The recruits had been kept squatting miserably in their foxholes almost twenty minutes, until the direction of the wind had changed and the rain was blowing directly into their faces. It almost seemed the exercise had been deliberately delayed until the skies were at their worst.

The instant he heard the signal, Manders began firing his eight rounds quickly and blindly down range, allowing only as much time between shots as it took him to cock the bolt of his rifle. He was trembling so hard that his fingers jerked on the trigger and the brief bursts of flame from the blank rounds scattered wildly in all directions. Falling back into the foxhole, he knew the immediate relief he always felt after he'd cleared his rifle. The thought that he might one day have to fire real ammunition at a real enemy appalled him. It went against his nature to the point that his rifle was an alien and hostile tool in his hands, a thing to distrust, a symbol that stood in so many ways for all the things about the Army he despised—the cold metallic repudiation of being, the ruthless disregard for self. He had to restrain himself from throwing the rifle into the mud at his feet. By an application of will he stacked it against the wall of the foxhole and pulled his poncho over him, then crouched down, settling in to wait for the simulated atomic explosion, wondering what it would be, wondering how anything could simulate an atomic explosion.

Beside him Ogden was hammering with his fist at the bolt of his rifle. "One lousy shot left," he muttered. "And the fuckin thing goes and jams." He slammed the barrel against a tree stump above the lip of the foxhole, jolting open the bolt and triggering the round in his chamber. It went off like a rope of flame slashing into the foxhole little more than six inches from where Manders was sitting. Stunned speechless, he could only shake his head.

From somewhere down range came a muffled blast, as if a balloon had popped under water, and the air was filled with an acrid, burning odor. "Take cover!" came a shout down the line.

Ogden leaped back in mock fright. "They got me," he said, laughing, clutching his chest, coughing as the smoke seeped into his lungs.

"For Christ's sake, grow up," Manders said. He grabbed Ogden by the shoulders and pulled him down in the foxhole.

Several moments were spent while the two fastened their ponchos together. Once finished, they were secured in semi-darkness beneath an almost airtight shelter, with only a thin trickle of rain dripping through the rip in Ogden's poncho below the pocket where he carried his bayonet unsheathed. The water splayed the front of his fatigue jacket as he sprawled against the wall of the foxhole. He held his rifle across his knees and, anchoring the butt plate against the wall, dug a live round of ammunition out of his pocket. He stared at it for a moment, his fingers tracing its smooth shiny contours, and then he opened the bolt of his rifle, shoved the round in the chamber, and slammed the bolt closed. The muzzle of the rifle was pointed squarely at the arch of his foot.

Manders watched him in horror. "Where'd you get that? That's a live round!"

Ogden chuckled, a lopsided grin creasing his mud-streaked face. "Shit. You all ascared or somethin?"

"You're damn right I'm scared. I was scared when you were firing blanks."

"What for? You all don't think—"

Manders leaned forward and grabbed Ogden's wrist. "I don't want to think. Now unload that rifle and put it down."

Shrugging, petulantly sucking in his fallow cheeks, Ogden pressed the safety catch on his rifle and let it drop forward in his lap. "Relax," he said. "No sense gettin your feathers up, fella. I ain't gonna fire it off."

"Then why'd you load it?"

"Just makin sure. I mean in combat guys don't sit around with empty pieces."

"We're not in combat. Now unload that goddam rifle!"

"Leave me alone," Ogden whined. "It's my rifle. I can do whatever I want."

"Unload it or I'll break your arm!" Manders said with as much emotion as he could muster. But even as he spoke he knew he had made a mistake; the hand that held Ogden's wrist did so more out of desperation than any real confidence that he could make the Arkansas boy give up the rifle.

So they remained for several minutes, staring at one another across the private gloom of the foxhole that separated them, until, releasing Ogden's wrist, Manders sank back against the wall, his eyes wary, sweeping Ogden's face.

"You all got nothin to worry about," Ogden said. "I ain't gonna fire it. See." His hands rose from the rifle, high over his head, but they were not hands raised in surrender. The beveled grin returned to his face.

Manders looked at him helplessly. In his cramped posture against the wall, the damp cloth of his fatigues chafed at him, but he did not dare stretch his legs. The floor of the foxhole was one large puddle, with dead leaves, twigs, tobacco scraps and paper floating on the surface. Vaguely distinguishable above the damp gritty smell of sand and mud was the odor of stale urine.

Ogden noticed it too. "Smells like some guy took a leak in here."

"Yeah."

"Damned uncomfortable. You all figure their atom attack is over yet?"

"We'll have to wait for the all-clear signal."

"Shit wait. I got a crick in my back already from set-tin here." Ogden slid along the floor of the foxhole to that section where the puddle was the deepest. He propped his feet against the opposite wall, crowding Manders. "This's a snap. This Army. I got it knocked."

"Either that or it's got you knocked," Manders said. He gazed annoyedly at Ogden, but the Arkansas boy only yawned and picked up his rifle again, caressing the barrel with his long fingers.

"I thought I told you to keep your hands off that thing."

Ogden grinned. "What can happen? Safety's on."

"With you the safety's never on. Now put it down."

Ogden only hugged the rifle tighter and let his grin grow.

Manders stared at him in silent rage. He clenched his fists. It seemed to him that no price was too high to pay for the pleasure that was going to possess him, a pleasure more intense because it had been building in him for so many weeks, a hot and wild desire to strike someone one strong, incisive blow—someone who resolved into Ogden. He brought his fists up slowly, waiting for the impulse to over-take him. But the tighter he clenched his fists the more his anger seemed to dissipate, until, finally, he opened them and lowered them to his sides. It wasn't worth the effort. That was it precisely; all action was useless, and there was nothing to do but wait, wait as he had always waited, and he would continue to wait, until—tired of moving him from one square on the map to another—the Army released him. He thought of fleeing the foxhole and leaving Ogden alone to his care-less fancies of combat and loaded rifles, but the simple act of getting to his feet suddenly seemed enormous.

Wiping his nose on his sleeve, Ogden yawned again and closed his eyes. Almost that quickly he was asleep, the rifle cradled like a woman in his arms.

Manders was incredulous. He himself was shivering uncontrollably and the stench of urine seemed everywhere now; it stuck to his lungs and eddied in his nostrils, a tang compounded by the mud and sand in the foxhole.

He no longer had any doubts about Vietnam. He was certain he would be there by Christmas, and he had a pervasive sense of what it would be like. In some ways, he thought incoherently, he was already there, with his nerves addled by fatigue, with the rain and the mud, with Ogden barely a foot away from him, sleeping with a loaded rifle in his hands. He had always wondered what war would be like, and now he knew. Worst of all, he had always known. It was exactly as he had imagined it to be.

He had not been aware of Ogden for several minutes, when suddenly the boy stirred and smiled deeply, a delicious shudder seeming to possess him as he eased into a more comfortable position against the wall and began to turn the rifle in his hands. He pointed the muzzle directly at Manders, his slender fingers wrapped in sleep around the trigger.

To his alarm Manders saw that the safety catch of the rifle was no longer locked. He drew a shallow breath as the muzzle leveled on his forehead and fixed there, freezing him in its bead, stripping him instantly of the casual monotony, the dull work, the saving depression, which had supported him like a cast during his weeks in the Army. Into the void rushed the sudden, sure knowledge that he was going to die —even now Ogden's fingers tightened on the trigger—here in this seamy foxhole under the most foolish and demeaning circumstances. It was unfair. It was reasonless. It was absurd.

Yet, even as he stared at the muzzle of Ogden's rifle, and beyond it at the indolent, vacuous smile on the boy's face, Ogden lapsed deeper into sleep, saliva drooling from his slack mouth, and his hand fell away from the trigger. The muzzle of the rifle lowered until it was pointed at the floor of the foxhole. Gradually Manders slipped forward, almost collapsing in the mud and the water, sinking in, hardly aware of its chill. Huddled there on all fours, he was overcome by a sudden languor, as though he had been anesthetized.

In time the rain stopped. The recruits were whistled from their foxholes, allowing Manders to take up again his anonymous place in Charlie Company. In the days that followed he was careful to avoid Ogden, and although he never talked about the incident in the foxhole to anyone, it stuck firmly in his mind, more illusory than real on the nights when he lay in his bunk and mulled it over, but prominent all the same. The whole thing took on an almost ludicrous significance when he learned that Ogden had broken the firing pin of his rifle in slamming it against the tree stump, and the rifle was otherwise so badly rusted that it was hardly worth repairing. Bivouac slipped by, and then the last week of Basic, and soon all the men of Charlie Company were dispatched on their own separate ways to their permanent assignments, none of which was in Vietnam.

So Manders did not go to war that Christmas. He thought about the whole affair in the foxhole with confused disgust and relief for several weeks. Then it sank quietly into the back of his mind, heaped over by thousands of other momentary disorders and breakdowns for nearly two years.

One day, of course, the war came for him, as he had always known it would, and he was positioned behind a machine gun, lying among the trees and thickets of a spring field in a strange village of a strange country, when without warning, sharply and clearly, as though he were looking through a frame on a scene that had not stirred or changed since his departure from it, the episodes from that day in the foxhole with Ogden floated before his mind's eye. He was so reasonlessly horrified that he lay trembling, the scene from the past so completely overlapping the scene before him, that for several minutes he was unable to comprehend an enemy platoon crossing the field less than a quarter of a mile from his position.

It was the first day of spring, and everything around him was a panoply of color. The smell in the field, with its coppices and ripening blossoms, was like the commingled sweetness and nostalgia he had smelled in the spring days of his boyhood. The enemy soldiers, as he watched them, registered as long figures and green and brown, and they moved through the field with such animal grace and sureness that he was astounded when, unaccountably, they began to falter, sway and fall in sickening waves, their screams even at a distance of only a few hundred yards unintelligible beneath the sudden thunderlike sound that filled his ears.

It was not until the sweet smells of the field were marred by the odor of heat and smoke, and over all the pervasive and inimitable smell of burning carbon, that Manders attempted to cover his face, only to discover that his hands were locked around the trigger of the machine gun in front of him and the weapon jerked spasmodically against his chest as it fired round after flaming round across the field at the oncoming platoon. Sobbing, he buried his face against the hot metal of the machine gun. Instantly the dreadful vision returned, and he saw clearly again the boy Ogden, whose simple, obdurate face he had almost forgotten, crouching again in the dismal training foxhole, again seventeen years old, smiling, sleeping, his fingers on the trigger of the loaded rifle, and the rifle itself cradled lovingly in his arms.

Grace Rooney

Death of the Father

Vultures ringed round the bed. Perched on the edge of their chairs waiting for that precise moment. The Aunt May, beaky, twittery, tweaky biddy. Print dress with tiny purple berries on a white background turned yellow. Can smell her acrid underarm. Sitting next to the Aunt Sophie, mammoth, her molten belly taut under the checkered skin of her dress. Broody virgin with coarse black hair frazzled by monthly cold wave permanents. Long raspberry-polished fingernails inflicting that black leather satchel that she clutches under her arm. And the mother, Lily, bulbous body, powdered white face over dark neck, nodding her head inconsolably before the nurse, white nun with ulcers, emitting redolence of bologna. Leaning together, their heads tipped to touch, like praying hands. And the older sister, Peg, tears sliding down her face, suck at her lips, sunken cheeks.

"Bahdee bookschick, you look so tired. It hurts me to see you like this. You shouldn't have come. Why didn't you stay at the game?"

"Stop babying her—she's strong. Be strong. Don't listen to your mother, Grace," says the Aunt Sophie.

GRACE ROONEY has published in the *Village Voice* and *For Now* magazine. This is an excerpt from an unfinished novel.

"She's my daughter. That's my husband lying there dying."

"Harom. Ungrateful bitch. That's what I get."

"Can't you two stop?"

"Sophie, shufee el whish, look at her face. Shut up, for the child's sake."

"Child? She's sixteen, smother mother."

"That's right, Peg. Take your Aunt Sophie's side."

"I'm on his side. Your constant fighting is killing him."

"He can't hear any more," says the Aunt May, her lips pursed. She wriggles in her seat.

"How do you know that? Tell me how you know that."

"I've watched many go," the Aunt May says solemnly.

Guttural sounds of wailing solidify to a whip that cracks, becomes a snake that flicks its forked, fierce tongue into the dark and silent corners of the room, becomes a current of flames that illuminates the shadows on the wall, rising, falling, figures of no substance, melding. She sees the form of a man with coiling beard and wild hair, pulling at the roots of his scalp, screaming. She knows him, risen from the darkness, out of the abysmal pain. A priest. Father, she calls, fearful, and he comes forth. His body fills the room, his eyes exploding, vacant balls of light blown out, eyes suddenly quiescent, staring with the debauched leer of suffering. She trembles. He moans and turns back into the shadows. The wailing subsides, dissolves.

The pink carnations curl brown in the aluminum pitcher on the metal cabinet beside the bed. A get-well card with a picture of the dove flying on a beam of golden light. An unopened box of Kleenex. A picture of the man Jesus, his voluptuous red heart pierced by a crown of thorns, his violent red robe, his lambent eyes, his cascading hair.

But look at him. Plastic tent ensconcing him. His head propped on a pillow, his face white and flaccid, his nose dangling a pink rubber tube like a worm of snot. His lips are moving.

She cannot speak. Look at him. At his puckered eyelids pulled down tight, at the thin cracks spreading from his almost invisible lips. Black nostril, an eye. She sees through it. An eye that sees death in the room, moving as efficient as the nun in white. Now shaven, the wildness under control, made more acceptable by a sports shirt and wrinkled slacks, the priest slouches against the wall, one minute sucking a long-stemmed pipe, then the next minute sole-officiating at a mimetic mass in shimmering black chasuble with golden crosses glittering front and back, and gulping down wine straight out of the crystal cruet. Dry-blood-colored sparkling wine oozing down his chin and it's nothing he tells her, not the first or the last, not the most important, not the most horrible. There's another kind, he sermonizes, a worse kind. The nostril squints shut momentarily. The priest winks at her.

In nomine Patris et Filii et Spiritus Sancti, Amen. Introibo ad altarem Dei.

Voices of the mother and the Aunt Sophie rise in anger. Grace can hear the words of the priest become a persistent sizzling underneath. And he becomes a nun in black flowing gown who jeers at them.

"Sophie, you didn't even let us alone when we were first married," the mother screams. "The first night you were at our door with your suitcase. Your sister Mary wouldn't put up with you the way I have. Share her husband? Her children? 'You let everybody wipe their feet on you, Lily,' he told me. 'Your sister Sophie shits all over you.' "

"Who gave you the money to buy the house?" the Aunt Sophie shouts. "I gave you and your kids plenty. And what did I get out of it?—Abuse, that's the thanks I got. Chuddah ah lakey, shit all over you. Ingrate. The whole bunch of you."

The Aunt Sophie is crying, sobbing loudly, her big belly shaking. The mother, tightlipped, petulant, smugly satisfied, prances around the bed. "You've always been the star boarder," she says.

Look at him. The black nun licking his gaunt cheeks, murmuring into his ear. Look. At his wavy dark hair gone white and stringy. At his emaciated arms, veins with the bulge of muscles. Christ how he suffered all his life. Making me suffer. Causing me pain out of his pain. Criticism—the Irish wit—ridicule were his words for me. He ridiculed my body, my mind . . . my sister Peg, his ally. She and I in bed. To me, who was pulling the blanket over my blossoming breasts, he said: What are you covering up? You've got nothing there. Two peas on a board. His laughter. Hers. My shame. They withered beneath my hands. Dugs of a hag.

And the cradle of my hips, my long legs. Daddy? Dad? His laughter. Hers: she looks like Gary Cooper. High pockets. No, look at her big feet—L'il Abner. His laughter. Hers.

Now nowhere in his face. An innocent. Like after embalming. Who is guilty. No. He's suffering, the mother said. Suffering. Wormmeat. On the third day.

Kyrie eleison, Christe eleison.

She sees the black nun, her sex indeterminate but for her sagging ovoid breasts, chanting the *Kyrie* as she rips off her cumbrous robes, stands naked, but for the heavy chain of beads round her body, black wooden beads and a shiny silver crucifix with his body sliding down its face. My husband, my Christ, murmurs the nun. He suffers. She flails her arms.

Look at him. At the pale blue bulging veins in the pallor of his arms, his neck, his face. The small mouth, lips thin, almost gone. No words out of him. Orange liverspots. Deathspots, he called them. He lifts his head, wearies, rests it once again in the pit of the pillow. His eyelids flutter. His lips move. He starts, moves his index finger as if to point to the black nun. He sees. Through the frazzled hairs of his nostrils, through the hairy eye of his nose. The pink tube undulates.

Dominus vobiscum, cries the nun, turning into the priest in his iridescent chasuble. Palms separating, palms exposed, palms together.

Et cum spiritu tuo.

Bless me, Father, I have sinned in thought, absolve me of my sins. Hear me.

You destroyed this man. The evil in your heart killed him.

My mother calling me, in the garage, in the car, always calling and asking and demanding and nagging. I was only twelve. She pleaded, her long flat breasts swaying braless under her dress. Help him. Help your father. The car door open, him sprawled on the front seat, his head almost touching the rubber running board. Disheveled, voluble. Swearing and moaning and cursing at her. Stupid A-rab. Stupid A-rab. He reached up and punched her on the arm and on the breast and she cried: Bahdee, let me help you, and he pushed her and she collapsed on the ground. Frightened, hiding under the porch among the damp dead leaves and pussy spiders. Her shrill staccato calls piercing me.

She sees the priest raise his hand, two fingers extended. He lets it fall to his side. I cannot; you have no genuine sorrow. It should not be the fear of punishment that drives us to ask forgiveness.

Suscipe, sancte Pater, omnipotens aeterne Deus, hanc immaculatam hostiam. Bells tingling in the white-walled, high-ceilinged room.

"Don't hold it in, Bahdee. It's better out—cry." Grace looks into the chatoyant glaze in the mother's eyes, seeing herself reflected there tiny inside the pupil, like a bee in a bud, a fetus in a womb. She sees the tears trickle from the mother's eyes and says nothing. She stares at the mother, at the wart on the mother's nose. It has tiny protuberances like a nipple which absorb the medicinal air of the room, the rancid odor of the funereal pink carnations, the polished aluminum antisepsis of the bed.

When the mother puts her arm around her, she shrinks back. "Don't. Don't." The sound of her voice is monotonous and cold.

"Your father loves you, though you don't think so. You Bahdee el whish, don't hold it back."

"Don't touch me."

GRACE ROONEY

"You're just like him—cold like his side of the family."

Cold. He was warm poking his head inside the room, smiling. After the cursing and screaming. Come with us, he said, come with us to the novena of the seven dolors. His rimless glasses reflecting the lamp. Me reading love poetry, the loveless. Leave me alone. See the pain in his eyes. Come with me, he said, coaxing. Shoes creaking in the stillness of the church. Black beads wound through his fervent fingers, he takes my hand. Like roots in dark earth. Later, walking with him through the cloistered dark of the snowy night. Streetlights like luminous moons in the black sky. Snowflakes like iridescent stars, whorling, the world electric. The heat of his sinewy hand.

Bless me.

Orate fratres.

Dominus tecum.

She can hear the Aunt Sophie whispering to the Aunt May and the Aunt May sighing. Their white faces glowing in the shadows, the two of them rock in harmony on the straight-backed slatted wooden chairs that creak cries into the quiet.

"He doesn't want to live."

"No—it won't be long now—Sister Amelia told me. He's on his last."

"Elbee—he was so good."

"His face—his skin is green."

"The poor children—I'm so sorry—the boys."

"It's for the best. He was suffering. Lily told me how he's been. . . ."

"Oh, elbee bee doot, Bahdee el whish—he was so good. He gave them everything they wanted—the bikes, the beebee gun, the phonograph. . . ."

The Aunt Sophie rubs fisted hands, like a child, against her eyes, inhales deeply, letting go a sibilant sound, a sigh. She makes the sign of the cross from right to left, bows her head, and mumbles prayers. Next to her, eyes of the Aunt May flit nervously from the bed to the window to the door.

"Listen to them, you'd think he was her husband the way she carries on. We never had a moment's privacy. Never live with anyone, children, you hear me?" The mother shakes uncontrollably, cries impassioned Arabic words of endearment.

The sobbing drifts toward the bed, seems to try for admittance through the plastic. The white nun glides after it, peers in at him, clutches the mother's hand, shakes her head. Compassion films her eyes and she speaks to the mother. Her skin is pleated at her mouth and the words emerge from tight expandable lips like expelled pits, small and clean. "A fine man. He loved his children more than anything in the world."

Lavabo inter innocentes manus meas. . . . A supercilious expression on his face, the priest begins to make the sign of absolution, hesitates, grins at her.

She feels the ebbing suck at her ankles, tug her down under the metal framework of the bed. And the sobbing seems to enter her body, and she feels herself gone liquid. The lights of the room twitter.

"El whish," cries the Aunt Sophie. "Jesus, Mary, and Joseph, catch her."

"Here, let me get to her. Don't crowd her," the white nun orders.

"She holds everything in. You shouldn't have let her stay here—seeing him like this." The Aunt Sophie makes the sign of the cross. "You Bahdee, God bless her."

The mother is crying, and the Aunt May is comforting her, cuddling her in her arms.

She can see the priest who is the nun in black wearing glittering robes over his sports shirt and slacks make the sign of the cross and put his fingers to his nose, wave splay fingers before his eyes at her.

She lifts herself from the chair and stares through the plastic, which like falling water corrugates his face. She hurries from the room.

"You go with her, Peg."

"A strain on her—Bahdee bookschick."

"Get her ice cream."

Running down the hall, crying, past the few strag- glers. A woman in a uniform calls her, reaches toward her. She darts past. She runs faster, faces sliding past her in a blur. Someone grabs her from behind, catches her, comforts her.

"Come in here a minute."

The older sister Peg leads her into the red-glowing candlelit chapel, where she can feel the warmth lap at her, lick her with the flickering yellow tongues of the vigil lights that hiss and whisper prayers to the stone saints. She feels warm and peaceful in the candleglow under the blind eyes of the statues—Teresa and Paul and the Virgin Mary, Infant Christ cradled in the folds of her chipped chalk arms.

Peg's eyes are moist. She flicks her tongue over her bottom lip, holds it in the corner of her mouth, and stares into space. "You don't know what a hell he lived in. His distance phobia. His world was shrinking; it was getting so he could barely go as far as work. He thought I could help him." She blinks back tears. Her face is a mottle of red light and gray shadows. "When I got my driver's license, we tried to go beyond his limit. His heart would start palpitating. He would sweat and shake. He tried to keep it from you and the boys. He was ashamed. Always making excuses."

That afternoon. Me, hiding in my room, listening. They didn't know I was there. All afternoon, the persistent drill of the ringing phone. His boss calling, wanting him to pick something up in Montclair. Them, making a commo- tion in the hall. Don't answer it, he said. Tell him you don't know where I am. Tell him I took the kids out for the day. The sound of him fumbling behind the bathtub, the unscrewing of the bottletop.

She starts crying and the older sister strokes her head. "It's all right. Everything's going to be all right." Peg's eyes scan the chapel. She draws her breath and settles back in the pew. "You should have combed your hair." Peg brushes back her hair.

"Leave me alone."

"I know why you're so defensive," Peg says, inflecting her voice meaningfully.

The chapel seems suddenly charged, afire, the tiny

flames making a conflagration near the shiny gold altar rail that threatens to spread among the pews.

"I don't want to hear any of your amateur psychology. Just leave me alone."

She turns her eyes toward the altar. The stark white marble, like a vault in a graveyard, is bare but for the two bouquets of yellow chrysanthemums, their spindly stalks rising straight up out of milk-glass vases, erupting in bursts of tawny gold.

Peg speaks: "He thought you were cold. That you didn't like him. You never let him get close to you. He should have forced himself on you. He should have just grabbed you and hugged you—"

"He never loved me. It was always you—"

Her body convulsed, Grace begins to cry again, gags, sobs, moans, trying to shield her face from her sister's eyes. Her anguish subsides and she weeps softly, watching the tiny flames like starpoints wink at her. Peg strokes her head.

"If—well, it's chemistry. You were born the way you are. You're very sensitive. . . ."

She can hear the altar bell, a faint and distant tinkling coming from the sickroom. The father dies, tolls the bell. Somnambulist, she rises from the pew, genuflects mechanically in the aisle and leaves the chapel, the older sister following her.

At the door of the sickroom, she sees the priest waiting for her, his arms folded, the wine cruet in his hand. Hurry, he says, you'll miss the consecration.

He draws her into the room, where on the long narrow aluminum table at the bottom of the bed he has placed his cruets and golden goblet.

Acolyte, serve me. Hastily the priest measures out the wine. She can see him lift the water cruet and she can see the light catch in the glass, a sparkle so intensely bright that she blinks her eyes against it.

Sanctus, sanctus, sanctus Dominus Deus Sabaoth.

"This isn't good for you, Bahdee."

"You don't know what's good for me." Grace avoids the mother's eyes, stares fixedly at the father.

"Now, Grace . . ." says the white nun, her breath

foul. She walks toward the bed, studies the face of the father, and slowly begins to remove the plastic tent.

"What are you doing?" cries the older sister. "What do you think you're doing?"

"There dear, now you know what I'm doing." The white nun touches her head. Then she goes to the foot of the bed, where she slips her hand under the sheet.

"Do you want to feel my feet, too?" screams the older sister.

"Peg dear," says the Aunt May, "come sit with me."

The older sister leans over the father, kisses his face, whispers in his ear, crying softly. Gently she arranges the pillow under his head and tucks the sheet under his arms.

Grace watches the older sister intently. She glances at the priest and pushes past her mother, charging toward the bed. Hands grab her. Arms of the mother and the Aunt Sophie restrain her.

"Get out of the way," she cries. "Let go, I said. Damn you, Sophie, I command you—I'm warning you. Please let go, please . . . oh, oh . . . you don't know what you're doing . . . I have to . . . You witches, let go of me." Grace struggles to free herself from the grip of the mother and the Aunt Sophie as she watches the priest mix the water and the wine and bend low over the table, murmuring words she cannot hear.

"But he can't hear you, Bahdee." The mother's tone is pleading.

"Yes, he heard her. He can hear me. Oh, your hands —I can't breathe. Goddamn you." Grace begins swinging at her mother and her aunt.

"Mejnoon. She's gone crazy."

"Let her go," the older sister orders. "Let her go." The older sister steps between the mother and Grace, turns her back to the mother. "Grace, come with me. We'll get away from them." She reaches out her hand.

"Don't you touch either."

"Peg's right, Bahdee—go with her for a while," says the Aunt Sophie, her hand to heart. "Calm yourself."

"But I have to talk with him."

"What's so important now? You never wanted to talk to him before." The older sister's words fall like a net around her. She sees the priest's arms lash out, then fall tight against his sides, himself constricted. Suddenly Grace begins pushing her sister and her mother and her aunts and the white nun out of the room, grabbing alternately for one and then another, hurrying frantically around the room, pushing and crying out "Spiders, you're spiders. . . . Oh please, oh please . . ."

"If you don't stop, we'll call the doctor to give you a sedative."

She can see the priest lift the thin white triangular wafer high over his head. His movements now are slow and considered; his eyes are wide open, focused on the wafer. When he brings it down, he hunches over it and prays. Then he lifts the goblet. *Hic est enim calix sanguinis mei. . . .* She sees him break the wafer into pieces. *Miserere nobis.* She weeps softly.

"Listen—"

"Listen? You listen to me. I know something even though I only went as far as the sixth grade."

Dominus non sum dignus.

She watches the priest swallow a piece of the wafer, then lift high the golden goblet before bringing it to his lips and drinking. He tips the cup upside down, draining it. Then he takes the supply of uneaten wafers, blesses them, and juggles them in the air. They fly like birds, doves, through the room, land on the top of the bedsheet like flower petals. She reaches for one.

"Don't touch him," cries the nun in white.

"I was only—"

"Why are you acting like this? Do you want to kill your mother? What if I flop?"

"Let her talk to him. Go ahead, Bahdee, talk to him."

"How can I with all of you . . ."

She tries to push the mother toward the door, gripping her arms till they turn white under the pressure of her fingertips. The Aunt Sophie pulls her from the mother, holds her firmly.

"Listen to me, Bahdee. Calm yourself. You can whisper to him. We won't listen." The women gather at the window.

Grace moves hesitantly toward the white bulk of his body.

"Go ahead. Talk to him."

She can't see whether he is breathing, his chest sunken and still. She leans over his face, examining his sparse dark lashes, his meager mouth, his gentle face, still and immobile as chalk.

Whispers. Go ahead, talk to him. Tell him. Kiss him. Now before it's too late. He loves you. He loves you. You love him. You love him.

Him strumming the banjo, making the instrument ring across the white tin-topped kitchen table, plunking, picking, plucking. His face red and sweaty. Frantically vibrating the strings with calloused fingers. Carstairs bottle before him, a long-necked jigger glass. The mother wrapping her arms around his neck, insinuating her face between his tilted head and pulsating neck, kissing his cheek, his ear, his mouth, all the time doing a little hopstep with her feet, shaking her behind, singing at the top of her lungs "When Irish Eyes Are Smiling All the World Is Bright and Gay—With the Lilt of Irish Laughter You Can . . ." The mother dancing, singing, undulating the voluptuous body he touches, he kisses, he paws. Come here you little Syrian with your wagon wheels and your clown buttons. Bausai, bausai, kiss me, she says. Enabhebeck, I love you.

"Well, talk to him."

"He can't hear," says the Aunt May.

He's dead, she can hear the priest say, pretending to comfort her.

"Don't touch me."

"But Bahdee . . ."

She sees him struggle to lift his head, his head sinking deeper into the pillow. His eyelids flutter and sapphire glints in an opaque blue. She sees his mouth move, and the dry lips separate into stalactites of chalky skin. His breath is fetid and she steps back, her hands clenched into two tight white fists. She stands stiffly beside the bed, no tears glistening in her eyes, no words bubbling at her lips, still and straight. She looks mean and cold and she tries not to feel anything. But she feels his fear, his resignation, his death.

Gone.

Abandoned.

The older sister embraces her and she wishes to snuggle into the warmth of flesh, but she cannot.

Whispers of the priest whom she sees sitting at the foot of the bed in slacks and sports shirt with pipe dangling from his lips and a glass of glistening red wine twinkling in his hand like sidewalk stones on a winter night. *Ite Missa Est.* There's no talking to him any more. I told you he was dead. There's no getting through to the dead. Dead is dead. But it's not so bad. It's not the worst kind. You haven't known the worst kind.

"May he rest in peace," comes from the bowed white head, from the full, shielded breasts, from the nun.

"Don't touch me."

"Cry, Bahdee, it's all right, cry. You'll feel better."

Wildness lacerates the inside of her head—the priest is thrashing and kicking and screaming and crying and yowling and beating the body of the dead father and pleading with him to speak and to touch and to move and to breathe and the priest breathes helplessly into the mouth of the dead father and into the ears and into the nostrils and rubs the heart and the flesh of the dead father and beseeches him to speak, to reach out his pale hand to bless the priest. I love you, mutters the priest. I love you and need you. Don't die. Don't be dead. His face is a contorted mass of snakelike configurations, his eyes are savage balls of dense brown clouds, sparks emanate from his lips, from his whole bizarre face. And the nun in white goes about the room calm and efficient, walks brusquely to the bedside where she draws the white sheet up over the taut face of the father. With a prayer she cups her hands around the shrouded mound of his face, the defiant peak of his nose. And the priest, relentless, untiring in his agony, grips the body, caresses it, kisses it, while Grace watches him anxiously, frozen, her dry eyes glaring at the body of the father, at the twisted shape of the priest. And look at him. Under the sheet the worms are infesting his eyes, struggling into the tight line of his lips, through the porous tissue, through the thickening blood, through the sinews and nerves, through the fissures of the brain. . . .

And the priest becomes the black nun who becomes the driven priest who becomes the naked black nun who becomes the throbbing frightened wild-eyed priest who becomes the black nun shrieking follow me, follow me, parading the family into the cool and clean, green corridor.

Richard Kotuk

Steve

My cousin Stevie was a real Brooklyn baby, born out on
Flatbush Avenue somewhere near U or J, I don't know. But
his mom and dad, Pearlstein, Pearlstein was the name, my
own mother's name (I'm from New York), she and his pop,
brother and sister. Well, there they were, born in Brooklyn,
raised in Brooklyn, his daddy drove a cab, then worked for
my dad as a cutter, always seeming to be just about to make
it and then all of a sudden my mother would say "Oh—you
heard. No? Mike's driving a cab again." Or "Mike's working
with some haberdashery firm." "Yeah," my father piped
up, "a competitor." So he went back and forth, always
moving around, but the family managed to keep on, he
brought in the money, not that much, but no matter what
he was doing it found its way home. Little Stevie (about
three years younger than me) grew up with his dad who was
above all kind and sweet if corny as hell and uninspired
or aspiring (he was satisfied in a way that didn't even
recognize what it meant to be satisfied to let things go and
enjoy them), and they spent time together going out to see
the Dodgers on Sundays, playing catch and fungo on the
street or watching TV. And a lot of times Mike just wanted

RICHARD KOTUK has written TV and radio commercials. This
is his first published story.

to be alone to read the comics in the *News*. The wife Alice was a devil. A real fatty. Fat under her arms, her chin, baggy fat under her eyes, fat in the way she talked and complained and always demanded things from him. Mike was a great disappointment to her. It was obvious (and it should have been obvious to her the day before she married him, swept up in the swoon of his kindness, the thankful, pitiful, acquiescent joy of her stunted childhood of emotions, blind to her own powerful neurotic cravings) that he would never be rich or famous or prestigious. But as I say she had made her choice and was fat enough to want to stay that way and since he didn't bother her she was content to eat and bitch and grow bigger and worse than ever.

In addition Stevie had a sister named Roberta. She was piggy like her mother. And she had that same snarling "I want I want I want!" coming from her all the time.

Mike didn't let any of this bother him. He let life go nice for him. But Steve was constantly subjected to his mother's screamings, warnings and punishments. There was something about her, something wild-eyed and shaking, accusing and staring that went beyond all reason and was scary. Scary! Think of the face of Barbra Streisand but with the flesh weak and falling down on top of itself. And the mouth ugly, twisted, spewing out a steady stream of vituperations. Well, that's how she was. And this is the way Stevie grew up. He rode the bus to P.S. 212, the subway to Erasmus. He spent hours underground concentrating on the ads, thinking not about much . . "Preparation H Shrinks Hemorrhoids"—funneling through days of dreary darkness —clackety-clack, clackety-clack, on and on, the train vibrating, caught twitching on its steel-runner roadway—the gray black, dusty, filthy walls crumbling by not three inches from his nose—chick-chick, chick-chick—yellow construction bulbs exploding every other day or so . . poor Stevie, funneling like a roach through some never-ending drainpipe.

He learned his lessons, if not well, adequately. A quiet boy, he didn't make many friends, kept the few he had, and they hung around the neighborhood, played ball in the streets at night. He came in for a kosher meal, the plates always too white under the food, somehow more important than the food, too clean, or was it the glaring overhead kitchen light? His mom didn't care a damn about religion and she kept an immaculate kosher home. Lox, boiled beef, tea with cream, that was the substance of his life. And at night the TV would flash on, Mike would sit there watching, stretching out, lumping his thoughts onto the jiggly silver screen. Alice too would view, sitting straight up in a hardback chair (ready to jump to the kitchen for cookies or tea, for tradition, her Role as Jewish Wife and Mother demanded she serve him if only perfunctorily), every once in a while (in retaliation) opening her mouth in a squawk.

"Mike, are you going to fix the icebox door or not?"

"Yeah, O.K. Alice, I will."

Stevie did his homework in front of the tube then sat back and took it all in. Bonanza, the FBI, the Late News. Come up. Come all the way up. . . . Double your pleasure double your fun. . . .

And Saturdays were baseball days, out to Ebbets Field, yelling and chewing Zion hotdogs. Once even shagging flies with Happy Felton and the Knot-Hole Gang. Gil Hodges, Duke Snider were the heroes, the Bums were the Good guys, the Giants were evil.

You have to get the picture of Steve's block, his neighborhood, his building, not a tenement, nothing rotting and dramatic like you'd find in Bedford Sty, and not a two-family either, nothing as elaborate as some people were able to live. Little Stevie lived in an apartment house like every other apartment house in every other truly mindless lower middle-class section of our country. The building went up and down. There were six floors with six one-bedroom apartments on each. The halls were shabby but not filthy. There was nothing beautiful about it. There was nothing dangerous about it. There was nothing really ugly about it except it. The roof had thirty-seven TV antennas. Yes, the building was exactly, nothing. Gray as gray as gray as gray. The house gray, the streets gray, the sky the air the wild wasted shouts of kids, the toneless, endless, death-rattling cackle of the old ladies and men who lined in beach and aluminum and deck chairs salvaged from long ago summers at Rockaway or Miami now transplanted to the gray concrete walks in front of the quiet gray buildings. Summer winter fall and spring, the seasons passed and changed but the streets the people the elevators going up and down smelling of chicken fat and faintly stinking feet of medicine and old people of decaying flesh and the fresh sticky smell of Good Humor Bars smeared on the walls by the furious hands of kids. No nothing changed, nothing at all.

But time passed and where you might think that Steve would have been atrophied, done in by this life, it was not so. He grew up seeming like that, a capitulation, a dupli-cate, schleppy cousin Steve from Brooklyn. But at a certain point, I can't tell exactly where, something, something wonderful happened to him.

Belying his mom and dad and sis and block and his entire life he got really interested—in cows. Cows, chickens, geese, bulls, potatoes, corn, artificial insemination, every kind of animal culture, horticulture and farming, the whole science of it. That's right, the boy from Brooklyn started to study the beasts of the farm. He grew to love them. He took out books from the library on them. He got a B in Biology. He studied in his room. And shut the door. Stevie told his mom and dad he wanted to go to college. And he applied and went to the two-year Agricultural School in Farming-dale, Long Island. After that he drove out to Missouri to the University where he studied two more years and received a B.S. in Farm Science. During this time I didn't see him, but from what his family told me he was very happy. He spent all of his time with horses and cows and sheep and learning new and better methods of farming such as how to rotate crops and what kind of fertilizer to use. Things like that. Maybe you know better than me. Let me just say that the boy had found his niche. His family sprung for the money too. And after he got his degree in Missouri he traveled down to Georgia to work for VISTA. VISTA, Volunteers In Service To America, in case you didn't know. He worked down among the tenant farmers showing them new and better methods to use on their small and sometimes very poor crops.

Stevie's sister Roberta got married to Alan, a television commercial editor with long sideburns, a pot belly and a wonderful and understanding mind. They had three kids in four years and Roberta began to look better than she ever had before. Like sixteen years old. She lost over thirty pounds, her face got pretty and she turned out to be a very sweet girl.

Even Alice mellowed some. She still snarled, but she didn't talk as loud and she smiled more often.

Mike was going along fine but then he got a growth in his belly. The doctors examined it and said it wasn't cancer. But it wouldn't stop growing (they were afraid to touch it), and he started to die.

We all came to visit him one Sunday in the fall. My uncles flew in from Kansas City, the cousins came as did the parents and all the brothers and sisters. This was to be a celebration for Uncle Mike, it was his sixtieth birthday. There was a cake that said "Happy Birthday Mike" and for a good amount of the time while he was in the living room I cowered in the TV room and watched the N.Y. Jets. Simply because I couldn't stand to look at him because he didn't look like Uncle Mike. His face was skinny, sucked in to about half the size as usual. The top of his head where his brain was curved way out like the top of a pulled-up radish. And his belly bulged and popped up from his middle. This was all the growth. He could keep his pants closed but it looked like he had a balloon under his belt. So he wore a robe mostly and sat there and looked out dumbly through the comforting haze of his painkilling medication and smiled meekly and bleakly once in a while but for the most part (I'm sorry if I'm repeating myself, or my choice of words that is, but this is very hard to talk about and I just want to get it off my chest), yes, he stared out with that horrible expression of a man who knows he's going to die soon and knows there's nothing he can do about it but can't accept it anyway. I remember at one moment when the cake was brought in all afire with the candles and as it was set down before Uncle Mike he put his hands on Joel, one of Roberta's kids, and guided him over between his knees in front of the cake and together they blew out all the candles. What wish Uncle Mike might have made then we all knew too well. But they blew it out together (I don't think Mike could have done it alone), and for me this was kind of the saddest moment of all.

And then as I was watching TV Mike came in to lie down. (There was a day bed in the room.) So we sat there together, my Uncle Mike's skinny face propped up on two pillows, directed at the screen and we watched Joe Namath look terrible and throw the ball away so many times I can't remember. Mike and I didn't say much. To talk about it would have been like for him to rip off the bandages and spend the rest of his time peering into smelling the stink of his growing wound. Then at one point Alice came into the kitchen which was right next to us and Mike said "Alice, would you get me a glass of water?" She got it for him, her face a mixture of the most amazing emotions. Collapsed, a mask, a crazy fallen-together combination of fear and anger and kindness, uncomprehending despair. Now she had to serve him, fully, without complaint or reservation. And she resented it. She had to take care of him and be nice about it, really, because he was much worse off than her, obviously, there was only one way for her to act, and yet because of all this she was suffering too, suffering as one does who has all the stops of her life pulled out, all the plugs that held the drain opening of her security so tightly plugged, suddenly yanked out, and feels the water the velvet soapy substance of her serene and unctuous existence rush swirling whirlpooling down and down plunging toward the bottom. Yet for all this, because of all this she rallied and showed a side I had never seen before. Her courage. She helped him, served him, she was businesslike, she didn't cry or break down in front of him. She did what she had to, with strength, with a hint of real compassion. You must imagine now what it was like for her. We could all leave, go home, put dying Mike out of our minds. Or like me run and hide and watch TV. But not poor Alice. She was with him every moment. She was with him when the company left, when the house was quiet and strewn with the litter of the guests, while Mike lay on the bed, crumbling. Minute after minute after minute. The toaster's pushed down. "No Alice, I don't want any more." The clock buzzing on the wall. "OOOhhh!" The face drops. She holds on to herself. I can't stand it I can't stand it I can't stand it! But she does. And finally, mercifully, he goes to sleep. She covers him then puts away the dishes picks up a book reads two and a half sentences then puts it down and gets undressed looking at his shadow humped up under the covers a car breezes by below the window she pulls back the cover and gets in turns away from him the lump in her throat eased melted away by the knowledge that sleep will erase everything until tomorrow.

Steve was driving home from Georgia, that's where the VISTA camp is, with two Marines. He was going home to work and help support his father and ease the tension on his mother while Mike was sick. (By the way I helped with some of this by transferring my credit with the Red Cross to Uncle Mike so he got as many pints as he needed. And if you ever need blood you can call me.)

Well they had gotten as far as someplace in Delaware on the New Jersey Turnpike when a trailer truck came barreling up behind them in the right-hand lane. The truck driver must have been crazy or asleep or drunk or something because he didn't even try to turn or slow down but went head on smashing into and over their little car, crushing it, bulldozing it down the highway. The friction from the scraping set off a spark and the car exploded. The Marines in the back seat were burned to death. Stevie was knocked unconscious and caught fire in front. Two other truckers stopped and rushed in through the flames and dragged him out burning. An ambulance took him to the hospital. The doctors thought he was going to die that night. They said his blood melted. That his kidneys had been scorched and weren't functioning. When the blood melted it seeped right through his skin. But he made it through the night. He lived for eight more days. We were told it looked like he was going to make it. We grew hopeful. On the ninth day he got blood-poisoning and died.

We buried him in Beth Israel Cemetery in Elmont, Queens. The night before the funeral there was a service at the Parkside Memorial Chapel, one of those modern places that looks more like a movie theater or a supermarket. The coffin lay in an obscure corner. The family and friends sobbed in the middle of the room and in an adjoining one. Mike was there, barely. Alice couldn't believe it. When we left for the night I was the last one out of the room and I felt very bad about leaving Stevie there all by himself.

The next day as we filed out of the Chapel (the Rabbi had praised Stevie well, but had spoken too long, was too fat, had ended with that same refrain we heard for Grandma and Grandpa, "You never lose the one you love as long as you love the one you lose"), that day as his friends from VISTA along with the family stepped quickly out of the chapel I again hesitated, out in the hall I turned around and went back inside. I stood looking at the coffin saying goodbye Stevie goodbye goodbye, then I turned and walked out leaving him alone inside.

We buried him that afternoon alongside my Grandma and Grandpa. The box was in the earth the dirt was piled up on the side. We stood around while the Rabbi talked and sang to us. He repeated his innocuous words about losing and loving. Alice walked up to the side of the grave and looked down at the box. Steve. She broke down.

"I can't . . ." she cried.

George Cain

Blueschild Baby
(an excerpt)

It's getting dark and still I roam the corridors of bedlam. I'm at 63rd St., on Amsterdam. Must make it to 81st. See me, all crouch and stealth, slipping softly toward a corner, well lit by a bodega. Past the Red Cross on 66th, the police station on 68th, faggots' 72nd. Turn a corner and out of sight.

A sickness comes over me in this twilight state, somewhere between wake and sleep, my nose runs and my body screams for heroin. It is an internal nervous disorder which floods the brain and short circuits senses. I infect the world with it.

I come to Sun's building. Looking over my shoulder to be sure I'm not followed, I dash in. They're posed as always, the other inmates of bedlam, pimps, prostitutes and junkie souls. Gracing the stairs like debutantes at the ball, all piled on one another, they stare vacantly into the well. Not in white gowns. Somberhued tatters the fashion. From the bottom of the stairs looking up, I see the dark between each gap-legged whore's thighs and the men's baleful red

GEORGE CAIN's piece is a chapter from his recently published novel, *Blueschild Baby*.

eyes. As I approach they salute me as comrades do, "Hey brother," and the bitches, "Baby."

I'm hesitant, nervous before my audience with the king. The room is silent, but they're there. I smell them. Bright Sun and Flower, behind the door awaiting identification. Friend or foe. They've lived so long in this room, even the hall stinks of them. Of sulphur, cigarettes and decaying flesh, a stench so moist and clinging no amount of air can make it disappear.

It's the smell of the dead season, fall, in a Texas penitentiary. One day it was summer and the next, fall full grown. Not a change in weather, browning or falling leaves. But the crickets were dead and dying, yet only a day before I'd kicked them up at every step, filling the air with their raucous cry and answer. Then they lay heaped upon the ground, small forms dotting the earth like dried balls of clay flung from a turning wheel. Their decomposition fouled the air. A heavy yellow mist, fetid and rotten, rose from them. I breathed it in, tasting it on my pallet, in my stomach, and wanted to vomit. Sun's room smells the same. I knock softly and Flower speaks. "Who?"

"Georgie."

"It's George, Sun."

"Well let him in, woman."

As always, Sun is holding court, surrounded by his crew of buffoons and servants who perform for him and carry out an order, stick a knife in a back or go to the store for eats. Their only reward the shelter of this room and an occasional fix. From his throne, the always unmade bed, Sun carries on the business of his kingdom. Flower is his woman, the reigning queen, she is dangerous and carries a switchblade to protect her man. She is lately out of the hospital, suffering from tuberculosis and heroin.

I ask her health. "How you doing, Flow?"

"O.K., Georgie. Was sick awhile with T.B., just got out the hospital. Signed myself out. They wanted me to stay six months. Couldn't stand it any longer, so I came on back. On the Welfare now, got an apartment on 97th St. I just come by to be with Sun awhile. We're not to be together they say. Ain't that a bitch, a husband and wife ain't supposed to be together. So they give him an apartment downtown here and me one uptown. But I stay down here with Sun and we go up there when we get tired."

Overcome for a moment, she pauses and nods. "I'm feeling good though, but that's only cause I got out. I need these streets, they're in my blood. I'm O.K. long as I can run these streets with Sun. Then everything's O.K., don't feel no pain, junk takes care of that. Cough and spit blood every now and then, but it ain't nothing."

Tired of his lady's monologue, Sun silences her with a gesture and turns to me. His head is monumental. It's large with close-cropped deeply receding hair, features strongly Indian and broken nose. He has the appearence of majesty, power. It's a joke, such a head on his gnome's body. He can barely carry it around he's so short and hunched over. He whispers so the others in the room can't hear. "How many do you want?" From deep in his pants fly he pulls out the plastic wrapped packets of bags and hands me three. I give Flow the money and reaching into her bosom, she pulls out crumpled bills, and looks at them strangely for a moment as if she were surprised they were there. She adds mine to the pile and shows me hollow breasts as she replaces them, moves to the window and draws the shades.

"Why don't you get off here? Know you don't feel like running the streets with stuff on you." Sun has planted a seed in my brain. I can't walk the streets with heroin in my possession, it distorts my posture, making me furtive and sneaking.

"Flow, get my things out. Georgie's going to get off." She rummages about in a box overflowing with clothes. Finding the apparatus, she sets it up on the table.

I dump the stuff in the cooker, add water, cook, and tie up. Then draw most of the solution into the dropper. I plunge it into my arm, popping and crackling as it tears through old scar tissue, then the click of a punctured vein and I squeeze the bulb. There is no longer anything dramatic or pleasurable about junk, it is only a medicine, a restorative. It is done, and the world returns to normal:

inanimate objects in the room no longer try to impose themselves upon me, they are passive now, awaiting consciousness
to make them real. My sickness has left, it's like waking.
Sun walks to the cooker to see how well I've paid him.
Junk is the coin of this realm, money is only the labor to
acquire it. He is satisfied and draws it up. There is a lull in
the world, a comfortable peace, all is still for a moment: but
awareness comes.

Head buried between her legs, gagging on spit, Tracy
screams across the room. "Georgie, today's my birthday, I'm
nineteen years old, we're having a party, right momma?"

"That's right baby," Flow answers.

"Come and kiss me Georgie."

"Kiss her for her birthday," urges Sun, and I go to
kiss her on the cheek. Instead she grabs my head and presses
her lips against mine, choking me with tongue and saliva.

"A birthday kiss. Don't try and fuck her." Sun laughs.

"Leave her go," slobbers the white boy, awake now
in the corner. I fall back on the bed.

"Tommy, wake up," Tracy calls to him. "Meet
Georgie."

"Hey man." Words stumble from his mouth, guttural
and moist. He struggles to keep his head up and eyes open.

"Don't I know you, Georgie? Damn it's hot in here,
open the windows, Sun."

"They're open."

"Take your shirt off," Flow says, and he strips to his
pants and begins picking his toes, sweating like a pig. His
white skin is covered with tattoos and shines like plastic.
It's hot, and I take my shirt off and begin tearing my flesh,
leaving long fingernail trails across my skin. I scratch an
itch as if it were the most gratifying act in the world. The
dope makes me itch and nod. Nodding as if my spine were
rubber, eyes closed. We're all sitting shut up in this room,
shut up in ourselves.

"How's the stuff?" asks Sun.

"Nice, real nice."

"Thought you'd go for it. I knew you'd be by tonight.
Told Flow, Georgie'd be by to score. You hooked again?"

"Don't know, haven't stopped to find out."

"Still working?"

"Yeah."

"Don't know how you do it. You need to give this shit up and go on back to school, I just knew you were going to make it. You were going to make it for all of us. When I heard you were fucking around, couldn't believe it. Georgie Cain, the intellect, big time basketball star, it was a bitter pill baby. How long was that?"

"Five years, Sun."

"Yeah, five years. Been a long time. How old are you now, twenty-one, two?"

"Twenty-two."

"How many years did you have to go?"

"Two."

"You'd be playing pro ball and teaching now. You always said you wanted to teach."

"I still want to teach."

"Why don't you go on back to school? You could make it."

"Been thinking about it, but I don't have it any more."

"Don't have it. Shit. You're only twenty-two, your whole life is still ahead. You're only a kid. If I were your age and knew what you know, I'd have it made. I remember when you first showed on the set, you were a fucked up cat, always talking from the books but now you've lived some, you know what it's all about, and combined with all your knowledge, you can make it."

"I'm like Flower, Sun. These streets got me, I'm hooked."

"You know Georgie, this dope thing used to be a hell of a game, it was worth the hassle when you had cats like Cicki Bones and his brothers putting junk on the street. The scag was boss and the time was light. They didn't fuck with you much then. But now they call it the dying game. I'm in it cause I can't do nothing else, welfare ain't enough to live off. I want, need like every mother-fucker out there and this is the only way I can do it.

93

GEORGE CAIN

Whitey wasn't letting me go to school or teaching us nothing then. But you kids got it made today. They're begging
for niggers to come and do things."

There it is again, they all want you to be a martyr,
cloaking it in the guise of personal success, you can make
it nigger if you try but the price is loneliness.

"Momma, I love you," moans Tracy.

Flower answers, "I know baby, I know."

"Ain't that a bitch. She calls Flow momma. Flow black
as coal and she whiter than white, and she really means
it. She and Flow live together. Kind of take care of each
other. Flow's sick and Tracy keeps an eye on her."

"Yeah Georgie, we take care of each other, Tracy
and me."

"No, no." Tommy screams from a nod.

Tracy shakes him awake. "What's the matter? You
dreaming again? God damn. You're getting to be a pain in
the ass. You ain't in the joint no more."

"I'm sorry baby, can't help it. I'll get over it."

"I hope so. He's like that all night. When we're at
Flow's, he keeps us up with all his screaming and shit. I
love momma and she needs rest. You with your noise all
night, I don't know what they did to you in that place."

"Yeah, Tracy takes care of Flow." The junk is having
its effect. Sun is repeating himself, soon he'll be off the
bed and into his little dance and Flower will sing, the
king and queen will perform for me.

"We take care of each other, Tracy and me. Listen,
dig how I met her. Was coming out the building one day
and the cop had her in the hall asking for identification and
what not. You can see she's only a kid. Guess he thought
she was a runaway or something, I'd seen her around the
block, knew she fucked around, but we'd never said nothing. Anyway, I walk up to her and I say what's wrong baby
and she says, momma, this policeman. The cop, he don't
even let her finish, but turns and looks at my black face,
then her white one and back to me again and says is this
your daughter. I say, yes, she's my daughter. I'd just come
out the hospital then, was looking healthy and had some

94

decent clothes on. He just shakes his head and says well she shouldn't be out so late and walks off. We been together ever since."

"That's something, ain't it," mumbles Sun. "Wish I could've been there to see the cat's face."

The white boy tries again. "Don't I know you, Georgie?"

"No, I don't think so."

"Georgie just got back." Feeling my tenseness, Sun tries to ease the situation.

"I just got out the joint myself. Monday. Did a nickel at Attica. Five calendars, it was a bitch."

Why doesn't he carry a sign around his neck, telling the world?

"Tracy's my woman, last time I saw her, she was a little kid." Extending his arm, he shows me how little. "She used to hang with my kid sister. I hit the bricks Monday and I'm out hunting a fix and who do I run into but her. She scores for me and we all got straight, me, her and Flower. Flow's a good woman, she got a big heart, but Tracy surprised the shit out of me."

"Tommy, you got money?" Tracy asks.

"No baby, I'm busted."

"Tommy, it's my birthday and I want to get fucked up."

"You're fucked up now baby, you don't need no more."

"Tommy, you got money?"

"I told you no."

"Tommy buy me a bag, please baby."

"I ain't got no money."

"You stingy cocksucker, I know that faggot you screwed gave you some money. After all I did for you, you won't even buy me a bag. Dig this creep, will you? Flow and I pick him off the streets, let him flop at the pad, score for him, bring him here to Sun's and he don't want to buy no dope. Tommy, please, it's my birthday, don't do me this way, I'm nineteen today, I'll get you the money back tomorrow, you know I will."

He pulls her from the chair. "Bitch, what's wrong with you?" They stare into each other, both incapable of any real emotion or violence. They're dead, even her retort was mumbled tonelessly. He feels in his pocket and pulls out bills. Counting them, he puts one in his pocket and passes the rest to Sun. She has done what he couldn't. I feel for him now.

"It's your birthday baby, so we're going to celebrate. Have a party."

He reaches over and turns the radio on. "Sun, give me six bags. Flow, get the works, I'm turning everybody on." There is a great commotion and Tracy hollers, "First!" She smoothes hair from her forehead and lights a cigarette. Proud of her power, arrogant. They cook the junk up and we all get off. Flow cleans the works and stashes them again, then sits on the bed next to Sun and begins nodding. Sun gets up from the bed and without a word begins dancing in time with the music, swaying and bending low. Like a snake being charmed. His grotesque body moves fluidly beneath the beautiful head and tells a story; it's a madman's mime, steps slow moving, drug hindered, falling low. It must have been the way people talked before the limitations of speech.

Never having seen this performance, Tommy is embarrassed by its frankness and turns away. Tracy is high and uncaring. She is still and her fingernails are turning blue. Flower and I watch his every move. There is his childhood, the marriage to Flower, the prisons, the police, the dope, his wanting what every motherfucker wants. He tells it all in the dance. The music stops and he is frozen in lassitude, sweat runs from every pore, staining his clothes, and falls to the floor. He's left us, somewhere in vastness now. Poised for only a moment and then crashes to the floor, groveling and slobbering like an epileptic. Frightened, Tommy rushes to help and Flower has a knife at his throat.

"Don't touch him, don't touch him." She raises the gnome, lays the noble head across her lap, rocking and singing in a voice tired-toned and weeping, sounding like Billie. She is a bitch singing love to her man. Tommy looks to me for enlightenment, Tracy is out and dying of narcotic poison, the blueness is stealing up her fingers and air passes gently though her open mouth. No one notices it but me.

"What's happening?"

Flower stops singing and cuts her eyes at him as if he'd committed heresy. I wave him silent, making him understand everything is all right. He falls back to his chair and closing his eyes begins scratching his crotch. Flower resumes singing in her blues voice and Tracy is dying. Flower sings well enough to be a professional, but she is old and no one but us will ever hear her.

Sun is awake now and stares at the ceiling. She sings softly in his ear and he smiles. Footsteps on the outside hall and she reaches over and turns the radio off, gesturing us to silence. Tracy can't make a sound, the bitch is dying. They come up to the door and hesitate, then sound retreating, stop, approach again and then a knock. He pushes Flower from the bed and sends her to the door.

"Who?"

"Santo."

"Santo, I don't know no Santo," says Sun. "See what he wants."

"What do you want?"

"Is Sun there?"

"What do you want?"

"Give me three."

She cracks the door. "Oh. It's you. It's Saint, Sun."

"Tell him to wait a minute."

"Just a minute, Saint." And he goes fishing about in his crotch and brings up the three bags. Flower puts the chain on the door and comes to the bed, gets the bags and receives the money through the crack, then passes the dope out. She bolts, locks and pushes a chair against the door, puts the money with the rest in her bosom, pats it in place and returns to the bed.

Tommy has pulled his chair across from Tracy and sits facing her, holding her dead hands, he can't open his eyes and is struggling to stay conscious. Leaning forward to kiss her lips, he misses, banging against her nose, sending the limp head flying over the back of the chair where it hangs as if the neck is broken. He puts his hands on her breasts and protesting even near death, she moves slightly to elude his hands. He moves his hands under her blouse, leaning over her like some strange beast, and tries to kiss her again. But the head rolls crazily around and won't remain steady for an instant no matter how he tries. He moves his hands to her crotch and she doesn't move, he tries to kiss her again but the head won't oblige. He's red and running short of breath and slaps her. The sound raises Flower. She screams and pulls her blade, forcing Tommy to the corner.

"What the fuck is wrong with you? Why didn't you say something? She's taken an O.D." Turning to Tracy, she begins slapping her to bring her around. But it's late. There are blue circles under her eyes.

"You up here trying to fuck and she's dying. What kind of man are you? You ain't shit, what did they do to you in the joint? Should've kept your ass in there."

Fear has cleared his head and made him alert. "I didn't know."

"Yeah, you just got out the joint, you wouldn't. You're practically out yourself. Don't stand there. Wet that washcloth and hand it to me. Georgie, get the ice out the box."

Sun sits on the bed mumbling. "Oh shit, that bitch better not die in my room, all those fools in the hall. We'll never get her out of here." He hunts his works from their hiding place and prepares a salt shot. Flower mops her brow, then her breasts. Tracy doesn't stir. I feel for her pulse. "She's dead." I'm thrilled by the words, how many of us can pronounce a person dead. She's the first person I've ever seen die. Sun shoots her up with salt, she doesn't move, but there's an ugly hole where he gave her the injection. He's beating and boxing her ears, but the head only rolls limply from side to side. Flower takes ice and puts it between her breasts till they freeze white, then strips her and lays the body on the bed. She isn't arrogant now, only

rather childish and vulnerable. I want her to live and silently I say all the prayers I've ever heard. Flower takes
the ice and jams it between her thighs into the pubic hair.
Then pushes it up her pussy.

"Georgie, massage her breasts."

"I'll do it," says Tommy.

"No, you sit the fuck down and keep out of the way."
We administer to her naked corpse for hours, till
we're covered in sweat. She's just as when we started.

"Let me try artificial respiration," says Tommy.

"You might as well have your way with her, she'll
never know." Flow is angry now, not so much at Tracy's
dying as the inconvenience it will cause. Dying is a common occurrence, it's the name of the game.

He put his lips on her, his naked chest against her,
and blew his breath in her, he did it for ten, twenty, thirty
minutes, an hour or more and nothing. He began kissing
her as if she weren't dead, rolling his body against hers,
rousing himself to coming. He made love, whispering, drawing from himself some vestige of life to pass into her.
"Baby, come on out of it," he chanted. "The greedy bitch,
had to be first. Told her not to try and shoot it all." I
could hear Sun in the back, pacing. "Maybe we can take
her out over the fire escapes?"

"Baby come on, ain't nothing wrong with you. You
just want some attention. You ain't no little kid no more
baby, come on wake up." He smacked her across the face
and rode her up and down, moving her body to fit his
movements. He began the chant again. Riding her belly.
"Baby, wake up. You know ain't nothing wrong. Just want
some attention, you ain't no little shit ass, are you? You
ain't no little shit ass baby, wake up. You're a big girl now.
I'm your old man. Ain't I your old man? Baby, don't do
this to me. Wake up, baby. Please wake up. Baby don't do
me this way. I need you. This is your man talking to you,
baby. You're my woman, ain't you my woman?" His voice
was soft and caressing. "Baby we got too many things to do
together, you can't cut out on me like this."

99

Sun and Flower stood conferring in the corner how they could dispose of the body and I sat in the chair paralyzed.

She hiccoughed and rolled, protesting his rape, and we ran to the bed. Flower pulled him off and began beating Tracy around the breasts. She hiccoughed some more, bringing up bile, and began moaning softly. Flower put the ice on her again and she began breathing. He'd loved her into life, Tommy had, with my eyes I'd seen him do it. He sat in the chair, overcome.

Flow threw a sheet over Tracy and put her in the tub. We could hear the cold water running through the pipes. When they came back into the room Flower supported Tracy, who was still blue in the lips. She sat on the bed.

"Anyone got a smoke?" I lit one and handed it to her.

"How long have I been out?"

"About four hours," Sun said. Then Tommy began.

"We had a hell of a time bringing you back, ice, salt shot, artificial respiration, took your clothes off." She cut him short.

"You finally got what you wanted, uh. You bastard."

Milani

The Meadowlark Municipal Dump,

sprawl of ruin, lair of untamed oddity,
tryst of a love like a thousand pale green moths
(fluttering guitar-shaped wings in the autumn moonlight, they soared above the smoldering garbage mountains,
wheeled beyond a pyramid of broken glass that glittered,
past the bathtubs sprouting sunflowers and metallic Christmas trees, over rows of doorless refrigerators topped with
fractured mannequins, skimmed the wall of rusty radiators,
surged between the rotting timbers of the caved-in spur-line
trestle, swirled above it, and became a silverygreen undulating crystalline ball, glowing,
    till the nighthawks swooped and sliced and ripped,
and left just dusty tatters falling to the cinder piles which
rippled toward the horizon like dunes of a blueblack desert),
    The Meadowlark Municipal Dump,
    church of the slightly tilted bone-white pulpit,
    began to nag the respectable element after they had
winced at the Polaroid shot and turning it over read

THE BARE FACTS:

REVEREND NELSEN

AND BUDDY BEVALACQUA

AT THE MUNICIPAL DUMP.

MILANI, a poet and prose-writer, has an M.A. in Comparative
Literature. *The Meadowlark Municipal Dump* is a segment from
an unpublished novel.

The next few years the nightwind, gusting over cracked commodes and charred tin cans and twisty umbrella frames, wafted moans of shame across the meadows and over the broad lawns of King Coal Avenue and into their bedrooms.

They hired a contractor from Des Moines to build a new dump, with cone-shaped incinerator and a garbage-grinder in a prim concrete blockhouse. On the other side of town, next to the Sewage Disposal Plant and Whispering Willow Cemetery, and as Meadowlark dwindles to extinction in quickening currents of Iowa going to cities, the spent and discarded remnants settle into those joining acres of rolling grassland.

An exterminator went to the old dump in the summer and gassed the nation of rats; escaped ones looked a hundred miles in vain for a bastion half as grand.

Flame-orange bulldozers gouged long deep trenches and buried it all, even the blue caboose; leveled Indian Mound that rose above like a cresting wave of earth; crushed the three forked elms on top and smashed the high thicket wall, just as it exploded into spikes and spirals of tiny blood-red trumpets writhing through the swarms of leaves.

The greasy purple turkeys fanned their tails and flew into the sunset,

the knee-high fire-eyed milk-cats slunk across the prairie,

a shroud of summer grass grew up and sighed in the wind, sighs each year above The Meadowlark Municipal Dump,

sprawl of ruin for Hal and Buddy, tryst of a love like guitar-winged pale green moths,

older than the town, some said, the Mound itself the dump of desperate Indian families racked with syphilis and pleurisy, huddled on gaunt farmland until the white men sent them to destruction on a reservation,

thicket trap for Hall and Buddy, lair of untamed oddity, of bitter blood-red trumpets,

grew as the town was growing, grew as the town was shrinking, many moldering acres spreading tear-shaped from the gaping side of Indian Mound.

"Past the junk and garbage, Hal, through that gateway-like, where the middle of the trestle-bridge has fallen in, railroad tracks twisting down from one side, a coal-car dangling from the other, and over the cinder dunes, beyond the night of fields and towns, is freedom—a chance, sheltered by skyscrapers, for me to be me, and that's where I'm going, soon as I can. But what's with you, Hal? You've sat so long there, head bowed and eyes closed, both hands gripped on the steeringwheel. What've I done or said that's made you so strange?"

"Nothing you've said, Buddy. Nothing you've done. And not so much because it scares me, thinking what would happen if someone caught us up here, as because of the doubts heaven sends me in this moonlight, because you're just sixteen, and I'm twenty-six, a man of God, if he still claims me, ah Buddy, for over six months now I haven't been able to pray. Have to fake it in the pulpit, even."

"But loving's never sinning, Reverend Hal. In your sermons you say God himself is love. And there isn't any age on Indian Mound, and no one comes up here much any more, at least not at night, and why can't you pray just watching the fattest moon of the summer—the way I said it would, when it came out of the cinder dunes there like a rubber peach—drizzle silver on all the municipal dump, light it with a light like our own strangeness, while the car-radio glows pale green in your face, and pours out a river of steel guitars all the way from Nashville to wash away our loneliness."

"Because it was given to you, Buddy, to pray to summer moons and rivers of steel guitars. I still remember how you said you didn't believe a tenth of what you heard from me or the scriptures or hymns in church, that you were convinced God was a glisten-black, gigantic electric guitar, floating at the center of the universe, strung with fluorescent cables, strumming chords and weaving melodies to fire the stars and planets spinning into orbits of forever. And I was afraid, and angered, until I realized you meant it all. For the pure in heart, the Savior said, shall see God. But I, with only faith, must speak to an unseen God, my Father God, although he never shows himself to me, my prayers to him drove away the shudders of big shadow birds swooping, trailing talons through my mind, and shiny leather boots stalking, thudding, in the pit of my stomach. And the danger flashes, from eyes around me, long as I can remember, unless my heart opens to him I feel abandoned. Out of control. Like in the jungle of another life. Before I took him as my father."

"And you feel that way now, Reverend Hal?"

"Not entirely, no. But unprotected. As if something awful could come out of the night.

"Like the people I've heard about who come out here sometimes to shoot rats. Couldn't they see us?

"And you told me about those high school students who go around with flashlights looking for couples in parked cars. Bushwhackers, you called them. Couldn't they find us?"

"Well first of all, Reverend, the reason we pulled off the road down there and circled through the fields was so we'd come up the back slope and between these forked elms. Above the very oldest part of the dump and Roman's collection.

"And rat-shooters would be by the newest garbage, way over on the right, and couldn't ever see your faded green Buick through the thicket wall.

"Even if they came out here on a night this bright, which they wouldn't because the rats can see em too well and stay out of range or back in their tunnels in the cinder dunes.

" (You shoot rats on moonless nights. Drive to where Roman's burning the garbage, turn off your headlights for a while, then flash em on again or use a high-powered spotlight. They rear back and stare at the light a minute, lots of em two feet tall, with long gray rubber hose tails curled behind em, each one a perfect target, and if you don't kill em on the first shot, they start hissing and running toward the light, which gives you a few more chances.)

"And the bushwhackers, you can bet they're at one

of their houses lying all over the furniture and each other, watching wrestling on TV. And even if they drive out, just look down there, how many times the road doubles back on itself before it finally disappears behind that hill. Unless they parked three miles away and walked, we'd see headlights flashing and have time to make it look like we were out here to shoot turkeys and milk-cats.

"Which is why we keep my brother Wally's deer-rifle loaded in the back seat."

"Well thanks for finally explaining that damned rifle back there. And the turkeys and milk-cats?"

"Look out there on the cinder-smasher, the black thing like an upside-down pyramid on stilts at the end of the spurline. Those big blobs perched around the edges are turkeys. Part of a flock of maybe a hundred that lives out here.

"Wally figured out their ancestors escaped from the New Victory Turkey Ranch that used to be a few hills over from here and had a big business going selling turkey meat to the Army, till they broke some kind of regulation and got all their contracts canceled and went bankrupt.

"But Wally could barely remember they'd raised huge black turkeys that could hardly fly and seemed like they were all breast except for a big fantail with white arcs like half a bullseye.

"The escaped ones had to look around for their food when they got over here, so they started losing weight and being able to fly well again and generation by generation they've been turning back into the shape and color of wild turkeys. Right now they're sort of greasy purple and still have those bullseye fantails. Live on garbage, mostly, and bugs and seeds. Supposedly contaminated, so nobody hunts em, and they have an easy life out here and just keep on hanging around and multiplying.

"And Wally figured out the first of the milk-cats came from some of the abandoned farms that are all over here, those pure white cats that hang around dairy barns and have eyes that flash red-orange when the light hits em a certain way.

"They started going wild too, hunting rats and living

up in these elm trees, and they've gotten to be a big family, lots of em tall as a man's knee and almost four feet long with another two feet of tail, and they drive off any other kind of cat, so every one you see out here is pure white.

"Right now they're all prowling around where Roman's burning the garbage, because the rats are streaming in from the cinder dunes trying to get to the garbage before the best part's burned.

"The cats stake themselves out in between, and the rats have to decide how much chance to take, you can see em up on their hind legs sniffing the breeze from old bedframes and dresser-mirrors and things, then they'll bob up near the flames, and all of a sudden you'll see a white streak, and tin cans and eggshells and grapefruit halves go flying way up into the air where there's a few turkeys flapping in and out of the smoke, and Roman's on the sidelines shaking a rake at the whole scene.

"Roman's the caretaker out here. About your age, Hal. He's a deaf-mute. Looks like the Jolly Green Giant, except his eyes are wide and serious. He lives by the side of the road in a converted caboose that you probably didn't notice when we passed by because it's almost completely grown over with morning-glory vines."

"If I did notice I've forgotten, for thinking about the size of the milk-cats, Buddy, since this is their home up here, won't it be dangerous if they come back and find us intruding?"

"They all came back one time when I was out here with Vernon Weston, the kid I told you about who moved away.

"He saw one carrying a huge rat, and he said the way her stomach was hanging down he bet she had a litter of kittens to nurse and for us to get out and have a look.

"And I was lots more worried than you are now, hanging on to Vernon, who was a big muscular kid, and we walked over, and sure enough she had a litter, in a great big lard-can stuck under a tree root, and she was in front of it tearing up the rat.

"I looked up in the elm trees and counted about

forty milk-cats stretched out on the branches staring down at us.

"Vernon stood there with his hands on his hips for a minute looking down at her, then he bent over and picked up her rat by the tail and swung it around a couple of times, and let it fly way out across the dump.

"Then he reached down and picked up that lard-can full of kittens by both handles, took it over to the side of the hill and laid it down, and gave it a shove with his foot so it rolled all the way to the bottom.

"And he walked back and said that'll teach em what human beings are really like.

"Well, all those cats just stared out of the trees at us, tails hanging down and twitching like they were nervous or embarrassed.

"The mother cat crouched there for a minute and hissed, then shot over the side of the hill, and we got back in the car and watched her bring nine kittens up, a pile of big white fuzzy balls yowling there by the tree root while she disappeared over the side again for quite a while, and then we heard clanking sounds and there she came over the edge dragging that lard-can by one handle in her teeth.

"Some of the other cats climbed out of the trees and sat around her in a circle staring while she put the can back in place and all the kittens back in it, and they looked over at us a few times, but I could tell they were terrified of people just like Vernon wanted em to be."

"Did you come out here often with Vernon Weston?"

"Not too often. And I didn't go any place at all with him after that night.

"See, ever since we were in grade-school I'd thought he was brave and liked me a lot, because he'd take me along when he'd do things like climb to the top of the watertower and hang by his knees or ride Doctor Weather-wax's palomino stallion bareback with spurs.

"But after what he did to those kittens I realized he was just a show-off and cruel and wanted an audience, and it's true I did like to watch him, he was so coordinated, had such a beautiful body."

"Was he the one who got you started?"

"No, it was the other way around. If anybody started anybody. No, there were others before Vernon. Mostly not important though."

"Mostly?"

"Well there was one that was important."

"Which one?"

"Roman."

"Roman!"

"For almost a year I came out to the blue caboose, we named it, because of the times we'd come back from taking a swim at sunup and all those morning-glories would be open, silky blue, covering over everything, and when they ripple in the wind it's like the caboose is floating on top of the wild rose bushes planted all around."

"Why did you stop going out there?"

"My grandmother finally told my father I was disappearing from her place for long stretches, overnight, whole weekends.

"And my father exploded. Said I was from a respectable family and had a responsibility to act like it, and what would decent people say if they knew I was spending my time with the caretaker of the dump, a deaf-mute.

"Called him a half-witted Serb, too, because he's from New Belgrade, which is a little coalmining town a few miles from here, probably less than two dozen people in it now, but when the mines were open there were a few hundred, all of em from Serbia or their children, and my father talks like they were idiots because they were miners, though anybody can see how wrong that is. They had the sense to get the hell out of here, didn't they?

"Well, my father got in his Cadillac with a teacher who knows the deaf alphabet, and they drove out and told Roman if he let me come around there any more it'd cost him his job as caretaker.

"I sneaked out later on to try to smooth it over with some kind of a story, but Roman had understood exactly how it was, he's so far from being a half-wit all he had to do was look at that long black car with all the chrome and the red leather upholstery, and my sawed-off father puffed up and poking the air with a cigar in a gold holder, and he knew the whole truth.

"He said he was sorry he was only the caretaker of the dump, and he thanked me for coming out and keeping him company and explaining what the place was all about. Because he hadn't understood what the dump was, really, he hasn't had any schooling except for a year at the State School for the Deaf.

"About all he knew for sure was that they'd let him live in the caboose, which doesn't have any plumbing and just kerosene lamps for light, if he sorted out the things that wouldn't burn and piled up the rest and burned it every night.

"He didn't quite understand the trucks and wagons bringing everything from watermelon rinds to mangled bicycle frames to the iron cage of stuffed flamingoes out of the lobby of the Iron Horse Hotel when it was torn down. He was confused about where it could come from so fast, every night a mountain or two of milk cartons and sewing-machine cabinets and newspaper stacks and ripped-open teddy bears and punctured galoshes and portable phonographs with their turntables flapping out.

"And he wanted to know every last detail about the things he dragged over to his collection, like the rusty radiators and the gypsum birdbath and the pulpit.

"I tried to explain it all best as I could in the deaf languages he taught me, and showing him pictures and acting out.

"If you can imagine that way of trying to explain something like the red plastic spaceship. See it down there in his collection, Hal? That shiny bullet-shape sticking straight up over ten feet with its tail fins resting on the four pin-ball machines pushed back-to-back.

"In the daytime it's bright red, and Roman keeps it polished like it was the real thing and he was getting ready to take her to Venus or someplace.

"Actually it was the main float in a parade a few years ago to honor the opening of The Onliwon Plastics Company's Branch Number Nine, which my father said in his welcoming speech was the beginning of Meadowlark's Industrial Renaissance, now that manufacturing was leaving the fester of the cities for small town friendliness.

"I guess you could call it friendliness all right. To get em to come here my father and the Boosters Club had to pay for the factory building and lease it at something like two dollars a year. For a company that employs all of two hundred people.

"And they turned the whole area around it into the Industrial Park they're so proud of, knocked down the old WPA bird and fish hatchery building and filled in the little ponds that used to grow fingerling bluegills and striped bass and wall-eyed pike, and they even diverted Wander Creek through a cement channel so any factories could use it to dump wastes.

"Then they put up those billboards on highways all over the state telling people to come join Meadowlark's Industrial Renaissance.

"So far there haven't been any takers except Onliwon Number Nine, but they're still optimistic, because Onliwon's been a success.

"Especially with their Handy Sandwich Fixins Stand, which is a plastic cone and a big plastic wheel that fits over it with holes for a red plastic tomato that squirts ketchup, and a yellow plastic mustard-squirter shaped like a hot-dog bun, and a green plastic bowl for pickle relish, and an orange one for sliced onions, and a blue bulb for chili sauce, and a whole bunch of plastic shakers for salt and pepper and celery salt and monosodium glutamate and I don't know what all the hell else.

"Plus they got an Army contract to make plastic ponchos for our troops to wear in rainy tropical climates. Maybe you've seen the slimy green things in Onliwon's display window, drooped over the two mannequins in combat gear flanking the autographed color portrait of the Army Chief of Staff.

"But they're proudest of all of their NASA contract to make the plastic bags and tubes they hook onto the astronauts to catch their body wastes while they're in flight. My father said in a news conference that even though it doesn't amount to much money-wise it's symbolic of Meadowlark's progressive outlook.

"I remember when I finally managed to get all that through to Roman with handsignals and stuff he fell on the bed and giggled so hard the blue caboose jingled like a sleigh for over an hour.

"We always had a good time, Roman and me. Like going to his secret pool a few hills over. He dammed up a gully with a spring running through it. Actually closed it up with big logs he cut, so there's a pool over six feet deep and maybe fifteen feet across, of spring water that's always fresh. On a hot summer night you can peel off everything and dive into water so clear that if there's a moon you can see the black and white polka-dotted salamanders chugging along to stay out of your reach, and lie back against the log dam that's covered with moss and feels like cool silk, and the water barely moves over every part of you.

"The back of my head in the crook of Roman's arm, my shoulder nudged under his, was like the missing part of me was back, whoever was inside me once, protected me and loved me then went away, as if he'd made a secret visit, even hinted he might stay, and all the stumbling feeling, all the looking and the calling out of darkness deep inside me dissolved and washed away over the dam in the crystal water."

"And I suppose leaning back on the dam there is how things started happening between you and Roman?"

"No, they started happening at the blue caboose, before we ever went swimming. And I started em. I wanted to feel Roman's strength, to wrap myself around it, absorb its thrust, even taste it.

"That last time I went out to see him I explained it was something special between us and never to tell, and any time he made a new friend not to automatically start doing everything we did.

"He finally understood, and then he took my hand and signaled something I still haven't figured out:

WHERE

FRIEND

WHERE

BROTHER

WHERE

FRIEND

WHERE

BROTHER

WHERE

WHERE

BEFORE

BEFORE

THE WARS

ALWAYS

FRIEND

ALWAYS

BROTHER

Jane Mushabac

Sunday

The flood of dazzling sunshine awakening her had drenched even the silliest things in its perfection, her quilt, how could she explain it: even her brassiere dangling lacily over the back of the wooden chair, the masculine careless lump of Peter's pajamas on the dresser, the green shades up so high their cords had turned three times around themselves. That Peter should have had to work this Sunday—and that her sister Fern should call—even the brief span of her own voice had rung true, "Central Park? Sure, okay. By the steps," against the residue of a lush sleepiness in her mind.

Alison had looked at her finished self in the mirror, at her thigh showing out from under the slippery blue and white flowery thin dress, at her brown hair curling long and soft over her shoulders; her eyes had looked elated—bluer—today but she had had to notice that the dress puckered unflatteringly around her breasts, and perhaps too much of her thigh showed, but Fern would laugh at her, Fern looked older than she did now, like a model.

Alison had had to throw open the window before she left and actually taste the brightness; perhaps it had only been an illusion. But from their sixteenth floor window

JANE MUSHABAC went to Cornell, worked for the Clothing Workers' Union, and is now teaching English at Baruch College in New York.

there had been no question about it; there was not even smog today, no grey mauve sulking around the horizon; today the tiny jigsaw piece of the river she could see between the buildings had been sparkling and the virile sun was shining so brightly the tenements had actually been glowing.

It was hard to believe they had agreed on noon: what would have been wrong with twelve-thirty, or even one o'clock—but no matter how fast Alison moved it seemed the people around her on the street were moving faster, for when she arrived finally at the park the crowd in the entrance was mind-staggering. Alison pushed her way through anxiously, drawn on by the memory of Fern's baby brown eyes, as solemn as a grown-up's, as if the small soft-skinned five-year-old child were at her side now, staring up bewildered by the crowds—like the time of the blackout when she had walked her two miles, all the way conscious of the treasure entrusted to her. Alison had to wait whole minutes, however—there was no other way—to pass the road where cyclists were speeding around the bend in an endless stream, in twos and threes and fours. She was already ten minutes late—it seemed inconceivable. From there she ran, crossing the grass around families picnicking, gangs of teenage boys, women sunning themselves in short skirts, babies tottering after oversized rubber balls.

She was out of breath when she reached the Fountain steps where another preposterous crowd had coagulated, loud and immovable. Was it a coincidence that so many girls stood together in dark wide-bottomed pants and dowdy minks with slouched shoulders beneath the bulbous decadent padding, their hands in their pockets as if an officer had said at ease, while children were running in and out among them, on tricycles and bicycles and pushing doll baby carriages between and in front of them? Had the more richly dressed men and women come together—was there a wedding on these very steps, that the tweed-jacketed men were standing like people from another country, absorbing small brilliant spaces of sunshine with such listening faces, while women in rich pantsuits and thick gold loop earrings stood near them with enormous dogs in leash, and others in shredded dungarees, white ducks and polo shirts talked, jammed in together. The police, whose shiny uniforms and bright blue helmets had clustered Easter Sunday looking midwesterners around them, were being ogled like the guards at Buckingham Palace; some bystanders had their cameras out and were stroking the policemen's horses, whose fine brown coats glistened in the sunlight.

Fern, Alison remembered with a start. Fern would be one of those people, somewhere in that crowd, lean and austere, so thin her twenty years would seem stretched out over knobs of collarbone, wrist, nose and chin and ankle. Of all the places they could have chosen to meet; but how could she have known, it was only April.

She paused only an instant, then she thrust herself into the crowd, saying "Excuse me" every few seconds as she felt her way around people's shoulders, behinds, breasts, dog leashes, dog ears, bicycle handlebars, denim jackets, suspenders, conversations. On mornings like this the sun would pour into their bedroom and they would dress, sneak out of the house to the island in the middle of the street with the fuzzy trees and thornbushes.

She cut herself a continual S curve through from one end of the steps platform to the other, and finally found herself going down the steps and to the fountain where she did the same, searching so intensely now she was sure she could not have passed her sister's angular face. Then she S curved her way in and out of the crowd and headed back up the stairs, feeling everyone was tugging at her as she wormed past; she was trying to figure out if Fern had come and left because Alison was a little late, because it was Fern who had called Alison, and so she might have gotten mad quickly and left—or perhaps simply given up, thinking it would be impossible to find Alison in the crowd, or maybe on the phone Fern had been more casual than Alison thought—if you happen to be in the park look for me. . . . But Alison stopped short between two fat men in vests; her stomach contracted; Fern had not said the steps to the Fountain, no, the steps to the *Cafeteria*. Of course. She started moving quickly again, nearly knocking a little boy out of her path. The steps to the Cafeteria, for some reason she had made the slip on purpose, it was not only a ridiculous error but for some reason *intentional;* but she was walking now as quickly as she could nonetheless south toward the Cafeteria.

Perhaps because there was a cafeteria by the Fountain and she had confused them in her mind. What was she to do, perhaps she'd just been sleeping, wiggling luxuriously under the comforter. And all of a sudden her long lost sister calls, is she supposed to blame herself if she can't respond like a push-button with immediate compliance, bang, would you like to go to Central Park, just like that, and hanging up so fast before Alison could figure out whether she was dreaming or not.

Dreaming: she was walking so fast now that the gorgeous weather was flying past her like dreaming. Gorgeous sky, gorgeous clothing, gorgeous children, gorgeous lady going by with a baby carriage overloaded with picnic stuff, a football tucked among the grapefruits—they used to pile up a basket to take to the island, with oreos and mallo-mars and toys and a thermos of milk which they would drink from a tiny tea set—gorgeous glossy tinted French eyeglasses fashionable as the baby riding on her husband's back in a papoose, and their two Irish setters, and a small brown monkey on a red leash.

Alison was getting overheated again, partly from the strain of walking so fast, but also from her intense gaping at all the people around her. She tried to glean from every face some hint about her sister—it was like speedreading with one of those machines that pushes the eye down the page, then asks questions, "Oh you must meet my sister," she used to say to strangers, although it was true, Alison remembered, that when she had held up her hand as a sign for Fern to be quiet, Fern had to be, and when Fern wanted to "sleep over" in Alison's bed and they would stay awake talking for hours, it would be Alison who made the final decision, and once she had even been insensitive enough to ask Fern to be sure not to wet the bed.

Alison thrust herself through every cluster of people, around a hot-dog stand, or girl sitting with her skirt too far up; she studied them as they studied her, as if everyone thought the park was his own backyard and was amazed at the number of brazen trespassers trampling every bit of grass and subtle breeze with screams and transistors, running, bright clothing, filthy clothing, body odors, aftershave lotions, dog-do, Jesus, all sizes and shapes of dog-do, she could just imagine on her white patent-leather sandals.

In each face she passed, Alison canceled out the possibility that she had perhaps said the Fountain steps after all, in each cape that her sister wouldn't have worn, in each inconsequential tricycle or presumptuous police horse, across each leash, she convinced herself that Fern must be waiting at the Cafeteria, yes, Fern was usually quite relaxed, Alison would find her there sitting cool in the shade, over a tall glass of iced tea, and feel ridiculous for the second stitch in her side. There her sister would be in a new hat, or bright scarf, her eyes an untenable reminder of the other sister who in growing up had disappeared. Fern would be calmly smoking a cigarette, would be poised, look French, 1930-ish, aloof from all the bustle. Perhaps an Austrian or Italian would offer to sit with her; she would shoo him off.

In fact for the first time that day it occurred to Alison to wonder why Fern had called. She was usually so self-sufficient, with her own job, her own apartment, her own friends. The question crept up on Alison, then kept pace with her as she headed across a long field where Ivy-looking men were throwing around a football and clatches of boys were playing frisbee, and catch and running bases and modified versions of softball, down to the umpire's mask and knee guards, but no bases, or was that soccer, that maybe something was wrong and Fern needed to talk to her. She was walking so fast it took her a long time to realize that she had lost her sense of direction, and in the course of weaving in and out of crowds and ducking softballs, and once a teddy bear some vindictive father had flung to an eye-popping police dog, the various clogged paths and roads had become the channels of a maze, and she couldn't tell if the day had lost its springlike pleasure, or really in fact if the sun were beating down so hard it made her nauseous.

It was as if she suddenly felt she had failed her younger sister in something. Not just today, but all the time. She felt in her stomach a certain heavy knowledge which she couldn't name, they had been so close. But just as she began to let her stomach knot itself around this knowledge, she felt someone grab at her arm. She whipped around to see who it was and laughed with relief. It was her husband's ten-year-old nephew. "Hi, Mikie, I can't really stop to talk, I'm kind of late to meet my sister," she started to say, but she hadn't caught her breath yet and he was quicker and spoke louder. "Hey Allie what're you doing here? Isn't the park great today? Did you ever *see* so many people?" His voice went up on "see" as if he were singing. "Hey, have you seen the sailpond?"

"No, I'm late to meet my sister Fern."

"You've got to see the sailpond first Allie. It's terrific. I've never seen anything like it." He had taken her hand and was pulling at it.

There was something authoritative about his sing-song voice, and his blue blue eyes reminded her of something, reminded her that she wanted something, but she couldn't think what. It was good just to be standing still. Fern, she knew, would be sipping her iced tea. She would be utterly relaxed. She wouldn't even notice that Alison was late.

"Come on, I'll race you there," Mikie said. Alison looked at him as if he were crazy, and knew that if she were his mother she would have been more reserved. But he took off before she said no, and a second later she was running after him, amazed at the lightness of her thighs and at the thirstiness of the breeze on her hair. She caught up to Mikie and passed him; he nearly tripped on two mutts rolling over each other, and she on a photographer's tripod, then for a moment she found herself following the wrong blond-haired little boy, and swerved to find Mikie right behind her. She was gasping when they reached the sailpond and the blood was beating in her head. He didn't notice but fresh and energetic as if they had just been strolling he yanked her hand and pulled her through three lines deep of people arching their necks to see the pond, and somehow she was suddenly up front with all the smallest children and there was the pond. She closed her eyes for a moment, thinking she was going to faint, but Mikie's sterling voice interrupted, "Look, Allie."

She opened her eyes. The pond was no bigger than a swimming hole but it was covered with hundreds of little boats with bright white sails, orange, yellow, red, even sky blue sails the color of the policemen's helmets; there were elaborate schooners too with whole arrangements of sails puckered out in the exuberant breeze. They all seemed to float so effortlessly, and it didn't matter what direction the breeze pushed them in, or which way they leaned.

"The destroyers!" Mikie exploded. He pointed at a few Navy gray plastic boats moving swiftly in and out among the sailboats. Alison had missed them entirely. They looked like absolutely authentic models of the ships she had seen rusting in some harbor. They moved by remote control close to the water as easily as water bugs, as cunningly as submarines. She soon became aware of another one, then another and another as they sluiced the water and the surrounding simple-minded boats, as they curved and dashed forward and backward. The whole pond, she realized, was crawling with them, making the gentler boats rock uncomfortably, and the crowd around stand edgily transfixed.

"Mikie," Alison turned and said suddenly, an ugly taste in her mouth, "I've got to go find Fern." She knew that he had already forgotten her. He was engrossed with the destroyers, and had already set his mind on talking to someone nearby with a control panel and antenna. A boy in a leather jacket behind her had his transistor blasting Puerto Rican music. "I'll see you Mikie," Alison said and wiggled her way out of the crowd to a path which miraculously led to the Cafeteria. She passed the balloon man, the chestnut man, the ice-cream man, the toy man, the zoo man; she began to pick up speed and almost didn't notice the hot insistence of the sun, the breeze titillating the long hair of boys she hurried past, the scathing pink of sunlight bouncing off tinted sunglasses, pair after pair as they went by unrelentingly; it was like a dream, this day, it had started so simply, just an exquisite day, an absolutely perfect day, and for some reason, after so much time of coldness, Fern had called and wanted to see her and in Central Park, what a beautiful coincidence—Alison gave the gorillas in their cages a sidelong glance as she passed—one caught her eye, and as if to spite her, brought his hand up to his mouth and began to eat what was in it. What would Mikie have said?

There it was: the Cafeteria, the bright new bulbous decorations like a scenario for a barbershop quartet—Alison wanted to swallow with relief, but her stomach wouldn't let her, first she had to find Fern, where was that quiet table, that island of repose where her sister would be waiting, first she had to sort her way past all the children, jostle her way among the husbands carrying trays back to their wives and families, being careful not to knock off the ice-skates tied to the backs of chairs—was there still skating—or push a baby carriage too far from the table it belonged to, or slip on the mustard some kid had just spilled or wind up in the line to the cashier, to the bathroom or to the polar bear cage.

Fern was not there. Alison looked at her watch: she was one hour late. Fern had been there and left. Fern had known she would be late, and had not come at all. Fern had called but it was as usual, just to get someone's telephone number, or a recipe, then clunk. Or had called, and said the steps, but it was neither the Fountain nor the Cafeteria: it was somewhere else.

Alison sat on the steps to the Cafeteria, oblivious of the irritated people stumbling around her. She scorned a man who leaned over to ask her for a dime, even though or maybe just because she saw out of the corner of her eye he was cleanshaven, in a turtleneck. A policeman told her she was creating a disturbance, so she took another look around the Cafeteria and left, feeling suddenly weary, so weary it was a relief.

Now she didn't care which way she walked. Now

she could let the sweat in her armpits air out as she walked, relax the muscles in her legs, breathe more evenly and wander directionless to find Fern. Now she could try to be warm without getting overheated—though she blushed hotly when she realized the man had been asking her for the time, not a dime—now she could gape as much as she wanted, and stare slowly right into people's faces, and their dogs' faces, and touch the tops of babies' heads.

How odd it was now to see everyone still rushing around her in all directions, pulling kites and quacking toys, and quacking children, to hear the clucking and clacking of the heels and shoes, of husbands and foreign accents and old aunts and opinions. Even people by themselves were busy with lipsticks or combs, looking into small pocket mirrors at their warts and eyebrows, adjusting their collars or skirts or bell-bottoms, or getting money out of their pockets, or poring over the whole *Sunday Times,* or *The News* or just carrying it—and sometimes losing half of it.

For the first time since she had entered the park, Alison thought of buying herself something to eat. How an icy hard banana crunch icecream would feel cooling the insides of her mouth, going down, easing into her stomach, she could lick the chocolate and feel the cold on her teeth, it seemed too much to hope for, a reward for what? for being late? for losing Fern? Had the man been trying to pick her up?

But the first three vendors she passed were all sold out, Eskimo, Softee, Good Humor, their orange and yellow plastic canopies and banners waving no less jubilantly in the breeze. She gave up after that. She was afraid of being distracted from looking for Fern; it was better not to eat anyway. Her feet were beginning to hurt, she took off her shoes and walked barefoot watching the ground for glass, then looking up to watch the faces. She passed the skating-rink and went up over the rocks and headed across the field, rejecting every face, looking for Fern's brown eyes. It was better not to eat anyway, she was overheated and tired out, icecream would hurt her stomach.

It was better not to notice so much either. If she

could let her eyes rest a little, she still would not miss Fern. If she kept them only half open, she could sift out the others lightly and easily and then when Fern appeared, she would be ready. She would be as casual as her sister. She would apologize for being late—and Fern would take her arm, and they would continue walking through the park until everyone left and they were walking alone together.

She remembered when they used to sneak out in the morning to the forbidden ocean. Where it was quiet, where there was no one. Far better than the island right across the street. Just the ocean and the beach and the morning sun, the early morning sun on the sands and waves.

Alison put her shoes back on. Everything was in its place. Numbly she walked past a happening, some Nude-In, or Be-In; they were burning park benches and painting the grass. They had impaled a dog on a stake. There was a whole brigade of policemen, but Alison didn't hear the transistor radios, the tambourines, the bongos, the police car radios, the rock 'n' roll blasting over the microphone.

She was walking along the beach with Fern. They were picking seashells. They didn't talk much.

No one else was on the beach. The gulls were screaming the perfection of the day, smashing clams on the jetty, scooping down to pluck out the cold oozy molluscan feast. Fern was at Alison's side following everywhere to the jetty and back, under the boardwalk, around a horseshoe crab. The sun was growing warmer. The quiet was getting too strong. Why didn't Fern say something? Why didn't either of them have anything to say to the other? She wanted to begin but nothing would come from her mouth. Words would spoil the forbidden lusciousness, she could not get out words, Fern seemed far away, Fern had no words, they were silent refugees from the brittle clatter of their parents; Alison started running home, and Fern followed silently. At home they had their breakfast, and neither could break the spell of silence.

Alison unplugged her ears. She felt old, the people in the park, even grandmas looked younger with their dyed white hair, their eyeglass chains, their rouge smudges; Alison's new dress for spring had wilted, was too short, too thin, the waistband was unwinding, she was weary but could not sit and stain her dress, there was nowhere to sit, no bench was free, no piece of grass without something, a dead squirrel, or small memorial stones from World War II, or a flock of pigeons eating breadcrumbs from a child's hands.

Alison found herself out of the park. She passed a long line of dark limousines and circled the Fountain. The sun had worn out its brilliance. The few faces that she saw had the sleepy look that fresh air brings to those more used to staying indoors. Alison felt herself gravitating toward the new tall building set back from the avenue, toward the streamlined whiteness of the General Motors Building.

There was something appeasing in its ugliness. She walked up to it with curiosity. Its ghostly whiteness, its long wide panes of glass, its monumental gross sterility, its bossy glassy presumptuousness; the whole day.

She leaned up against the great white building. The flashy white cars turned eerily on giant platforms. She stood alone transfixed, as the crowd had stood transfixed by the destroyers. Their white diamond extravagance, the gray plastic crudity, it was all the same. Alison saw her face in the glass (now she needed only to think about tokens for the subway, a dime for the phone, what to cook for dinner) ; she saw her plain eyes, plain nose, plain mouth in the glass, and beyond them and through them, the white cars turning; she was staring at her own brown eyes, steady transparencies, when she heard a quiet voice behind her say "Your sister Fern is gone."

George Blecher

Monterose's Story

1956, and J.R. Monterose is a smooth, lean eighteen summers. The scene is clean, everything is swinging, he has the
motherfucking world knocked out. Picking up some good
coins playing the tubs at the Club Montevideo. Wailing a
fine little cunt named Miriam, who says to J.R. in the hot
nights, "Don't ever quit me, J.R. I'd die if you did." And he
has little to do with the uptown scene. He has his own place
downtown, he's learned to keep his feelings way down and
cool it.

But one night, as he's walking home from his gig at
the Montevideo with Miriam on his arm, he hears all of a
sudden the Overlord of the Dragons speaking to him in a
gentle, bewildered voice, confused and on the verge of
tears: "J.R., don't you know we love you, baby, even though
you ain't shit no more?"

Calvin has to be putting him on, rapping his cynical
bullshit, but J.R. can't find a trace of sarcasm in that voice.
He is astonished. "Man, what did you say?"

"Honey, I didn't say nothing."

"You stupid bitch, shut up. Calvin, what did you
say?"

GEORGE BLECHER teaches English and creative writing at
Lehman College of the City University. *Monterose's Story* is part
of a longer work.

"Calvin who?"

"Calvin," he shouts, "I'm *talking* to you! I know you're here! I'm going to kill you, man, for opening your fat lip!"

He whirls around in the street. Nothing but a few cats doing little bopping steps in front of a bar, grinning back at him. "Calvin, come out here! Say it to my face!"

Miriam puts her arms around him and swells against him, a fine big bird, a wild turkey, and she tries to kiss him but he tears her arms away and shouts into the shadows, "Calvin, COME OUT HERE!" He picks up a bottle from the street and throws it through a store-window where he sees Calvin's face. Miriam starts crying and holding his hands by his sides. "Oh honey, baby, what's wrong with you? What's happening to you?"

Monterose laughs at the hole in the window. "See, Calvin, I told you I'd get you. You don't bullshit J.R. and stay happy!"

Later, much later, Monterose wakes and looks out the window at the rusty sky. Never a star, he thinks, and he glances at Miriam by his side. Tonight she cried and laughed and cried and said, "Oh, J.R., I can't stand the goodness," until she fell asleep smiling. But her voice scared him when it was so much inside her, down a little corridor of her throat, for he'd realized that he was trying to kill her. He'd tried to stick it through her, but it just got lost in that big white space and he felt three inches tall.

He gets up and starts pacing by the window, remembering Calvin's words: "Don't you know we love you, baby, even though you ain't shit no more?" He sees Calvin smile that melancholy smile, and he thinks: Man, what right have you got to say that to me? You know I was the best bopper in the Dragons. You got no quarrel with me just because I split. I was tired, that's all. And what is going to happen to you when you get too old and you get caught sticking up some liquor store? Or you knock up some chick and marry her and get a job stacking crates in that liquor store the rest of your life?

But just for your information, Calvin, someday soon

I'm going to split this scene for good. I mean just walk down the avenue into the park without looking back. Say Fuck it to everything, *everything* you dig? Because nobody, not even this chick so tender and loving she makes me want to cry sometimes, knows me, and nobody's about to. So I got to find something different. I don't know what it is yet, but I know what you're into ain't shit. And Calvin, you're just too dumb to know it. You're too busy showing the punks who's boss, strutting your ass off and telling the people who you are. And who are you, man? I'm asking you, baby, who are you? Nobody. You're born in shit and you're going to die in it. But not me. When I leave, nobody's going to lay a hand on me because I'm not looking back. Because you're dead if you do.

Miriam awakens and wipes her hand across her eyes. She turns and looks at him with one eye open, a little black coal. And reaches out for him to sit beside her. "You're all wet, baby," she says. "All . . . wet." "Yeah, yeah, go to sleep, Miriam," he says. She sighs like a trough in the waves, and floats back home.

Soon J.R. is dressing, scrambling around the room for the shoes and the underwear and the tie, trying to keep it quiet, but his clothes are all over, he can only find his pants and his shoes. But there's no time for the rest; something is shoving him right out the door. He stops for a moment by Miriam, snoring her cute little snore, her body puffing out the bedsheets like mountains under the snow. And leaves.

He is out in the street now, heading uptown. Almost sober now, but there's still a terrible ringing in his ears. He starts running, his shoes flapping against his soles, the taps clicking in the great silence. And crushes his fingers into his palms, knowing that he's going to kill Calvin once and for all, knock him once on the head, stick him and lay him out. To kill Calvin. But to kill him better than he would kill me.

Suddenly he is before the door to his mother's house. Go in, he says to himself. Go in and see her for the last time. Bitch or no bitch, go in to see if she's changed. Get a sign of where to go, what you are, all the shit rattling around inside you.

She was all there was. His father had left a long time before this particular night. J.R. had seen him last when he was ten, when his father brought him a chess set, arranged the pieces with a meticulous eye, and started to explain the game: "So these are the pieces and this is how they move. You can make lots of moves, but you got to make all the right ones or the other cat if he's smart enough whips your ass."

"Billy, why do you bring him something like that instead of something he could understand?" The voice from the powder-room.

And his father Billy, the man with whom he shared those wide-open eyes, the ones that made him look perpetually surprised, looked at her and said, "You're still as stupid as ever, aren't you? You could live to be a hundred and you still wouldn't learn a thing. But maybe J.R. can see where it's at, that each one of these pieces is life and death to the others, and you're the boss of the whole scene. You're stuck with the whole thing, don't you see? Nobody moves the King and Queen and you just make the little baby moves. You make the wrong little baby moves and your King gets it and that's the end of the game."

His mother was sipping at a Ballantine after Billy had gone. She looked at J.R. with a pain in her eyes that almost broke his heart, but all she said was "J.R., I want you to learn that game like your father told you." Just that, not another word until she picked herself up out of the chair, slipped into a dress where you could see the warm valley between her titties, and waited, staring out the window, until the next cat came to pick her up. And three years later, Billy was dying in St. Luke's, screaming for water, as they cut him open and saw his liver, swollen and rotten, twice the normal size, the liver of an eighty-year-old wino.

J.R. steps up the stairs as if a noise would bring down the walls around him. The hallway is dark, but every step is familiar. Sixty-three steps, the twenty-eighth cracked, the banister on the third-floor landing with a little carving, "J.R. is the King." He pushes the door open in the smell of her body, the chair covers with the flamboyantly blue printed flowers, pineapples and chocolate and the smooth smell of film-romance magazines. She hears him and steps into the kitchen light, still rubbing her eyes. She knows who it is, but still says, "Who is it this time of night?"

He sits down at the table. "It's the sweet Lord Jesus."

She clears the sleep from her eyes and stares at him. Looking good for her age, a nice hunk of ass bulging from her bathrobe. But she shakes her head from side to side when she sees him, and he thinks: Momma, why do you nod at me that way? I'm just here to say hello and see if you know me. Ain't that worth more than a nod? A twitch of the lip maybe?

"So what are you doing here, Jerrold?"

"Just came to say hello. Welcome me, Momma."

"Welcome you? You want me to roll out the red carpet just because my son Jerrold has come home at last?"

"I'm not asking for no red carpet, but you can do better than you're doing."

She sighs. "Argue with me in the daytime, Jerrold. Right now I'm tired." She was tired, but she looked him over to see if somebody had done a job on him and he was back to get patched up. But she knew nobody had done a job on him yet.

"Why don't you have your shirt on?" she asked.

"It's cooler that way, Momma. But you do look terrible, that's for sure. Maybe you better go back to sleep."

She sits down opposite him at the table. From her the fine thin nose, the long, lazy fingers. Which she spreads out on the table. "Have you had something to eat?"

"Yeah, I ate. But you could throw on a couple of eggs if you like." To make her feel wanted.

Dreamily, she rises and breaks the eggs in the skillet, stands with her back to him. The eggs plop into bacon-fat. Two yellow eyes must be looking back at her and making her nervous. Two eggs was a mistake. Three maybe, to show her his appetite is still good. Or one, to be polite. But not two, never two.

"You need money, I guess."

"I don't need money."

"You got yourself into trouble."

"No, trouble don't knock at my door."

She turns to him. Nervous from the staring eggs. And he thinks: I want to kiss out the weakness in her eyes and tell her she has me through all the shit of her little life, too much for her alone to handle. Momma, I know life is hard for you. Don't you think I know it? You ask me why I came? Don't you know? Don't you have it in your pin brain to make a guess?

"Then why *did* you come?"

"I told you. To pay you a little visit."

He sees her redden and start to anger. Finally, finally!

"Don't you *talk* to me like that, Jerrold! I had enough of your big-shot talk. You're such a big-shot you decided you didn't need me any more! Now something happens, I don't know what, and you come running back. But why? What did you *do*?"

Momma, poor stupid Momma. Don't you know it's you who needs me? J.R. crosses his legs. "Yeah, well, I just wanted to know."

"What?"

"Just that you're thinking and being just like always."

"I could hit you for that."

Hit me then, Momma. But her sigh is grand and hopeless.

"I did something wrong in bringing you up. I did do something wrong."

That I can't answer, Momma. It's too hard for me. "No, you did everything just right. You know that." He tries to smile at her.

"Don't give me your father's wise-ass smile!"

"You wouldn't want me to be exactly like you, Momma, would you? I had to take a little from Daddy."

A voice from the bedroom. "Baby, who're you talking to?" At just the wrong time.

"Nobody. Just my son. Go back to sleep."

Go to sleep, Faceless, go to sleep. I made a mistake and I admit it. Because I don't know the answer I'm after. "I better go," he says.

She's crying. "Jerrold, you can sleep here if you want to. That's just Horace. You know him. I'm not making you stay, but you can if you want to. There's a bed if you want it."

Don't say it that way, Momma. Force me if you want to. Wrap your long fingers around my heart if you want to. You just moved your pawn two spaces forward, now you're moving it one space back. The baby moves count, don't you remember?

"I can't make it," he says. "You got business here."

"Keep on hurting me if you like. But aren't you going to eat the eggs at least?" The tears on her face are as slick as ice.

"I better go, Momma. Don't worry too much."

He gets up quickly so he can avoid her crying and is out the door. In his head, he sees the eggs staring back at her.

Relieved, he walks the two blocks uptown to the old condemned wooden house. Where Calvin must be waiting. In the house called Horror House, the name Calvin's brainstorm—"to put a scare in the hearts of those motherfuckers, whoever and how many they may be." The rusty sky lights his way through the slat in the fence, the vacant lot of dried dandelions, beer cans, mountains of newspaper, old skins, and he watches Horror House loom blood-red before him against the sky. It seems to expand, to take a breath before he enters: "Don't you know we love you, J.R. . . . ?" He takes the four steps without a sound. And walks into the mouth of Horror House.

No one is there. No one at all. He tries each door, but the rooms are dark as death. Plague has hit Horror House. The Angel of Death has knocked on your door, thinks J.R., and for the first time tonight he smiles. But not so much. You don't smile too much about a thing like that, any more than you smile when the grandfather you hated finally kicks. You think the one nice thought you can think about him. And if you can't find one, you think it's sad that some cat has lived seventy-eight years without doing one decent thing to leave behind. So he thinks of clear spring afternoons sitting in the clubhouse with Calvin and the boys drinking Sneaky Pete and listening to sides on the radio. For he knows that though the downstairs is empty, Calvin is in there someplace. He must be, he has to be, he's the captain on the sinking ship.

J.R. walks up to the top floor. There, by a sole lighted candle, black crepe over the window, lies Calvin spread over the bed. He wiggles his bare toes at J.R. and rises slowly, vaguely, out of sleep. "Yeah, J.R., I knew you'd make it up here sooner or later."

"Yeah, well I'm here, Calvin. As you can see."

"Mmmhmm."

They sit and stare at each other. J.R. lifts his eyes from Calvin's face and surveys the room. It's not his any more. Filled with Calvin's personal stink.

"Looks pretty good to you, J.R.?"

"No man, you're the same nasty slob like always."

Calvin's laugh slices through the air. The candle-light trembles. "J.R., you're the same snide motherfucker like always. Dig, I know it's against all your principles, clean-liver that you are, but I got a good taste tonight, real Panama red, and I'm offering you some if you want it."

He holds out the joint to J.R. "Come on, my friend, it ain't going to hurt you."

J.R. lights it, draws in a deep breath and holds it, then gives it back to Calvin. "Ain't that mellow, my friend?" Even from the first toke J.R. gets a buzz; his eyes, little hummingbirds, rest on each object in the room. "Don't you think I'm the perfect host?" As they pass the joint, J.R. relaxes. He is King again. He has time. Calvin is not a bad cat, but he will kill him anyway when the time comes. "So how you making it, Calvin?"

"Can't complain. Can't complain. How you making it, my friend?"

"I'm copping."

"Glad to hear it. I've always been a little concerned that you weren't getting it regular. And that's no good you know. You get pimples if you don't. And I worry about your complexion, I really do. And how does it feel to be a big-time drummer-man?"

"It's mellow."

"That's just fine. But I suppose my next question is what are you doing up here?"

J.R. stretches his feet. "Calvin, I been missing you so much, you being my man and all, I just thought I'd drop up and see if you're taking care of yourself."

"That's sweet thinking, J.R. Friends is friends forever and eternity, no matter what little differences may tear them apart. Ain't that right, J.R.?"

"That's why I'm here, Calvin."

J.R. sees the two pillows on the bed. And the thought he has not let slip out this night finally breaks through. Calvin sees him eyeing the pillows, and he laughs again. "Hey, J.R., you should've let us know you were coming and we'd have baked a cake. I would've told Irene to be sure to be here, and we'd have had a little welcome-home-stranger party for you. Oh yeah, it's a shame you didn't give us a little time." He starts to shape his thoughts in the air with his hands. "Oh, I can see it all now. You should've come on your birthday, dig, and then we'd dress you up in your little birthday beanie and you could blow out all the little candles. Irene would've baked the cake of her life, I guarantee it. With pink icing and yellow letters reading, 'Welcome Home, Motherfucker.' "

It is time now, he thinks. You've said it, Calvin. You've said just what I was waiting for. He takes the knife out of his pocket and snaps it open.

But Calvin only smiles. "You let me down, my friend. You really disappoint me. I thought you were above that movie shit. But I guess you ain't, and that's too bad. You did have a hard life, didn't you? You just couldn't take a little kidding, could you baby? Now I don't have a weapon to my name, as you can see." He spreads out his great open hands, the pink palms, in front of J.R.'s face. "I'm just a poor defenseless motherfucker ready to take my medicine from the best Warlord the Dragons ever had. We were deeply sorry to see you go, J.R., but I guess that's life. What's left of it for me." Calvin's swan-song, played for the back row. "So . . ." He glances around the room one last time and grins. "So all I can do is offer my apologies and introduce you to the new Warlord of the Dragons."

And J.R. turns, too late, but fast enough to see Ellwood Nelson bring a lead pipe down over his head.

You may lay three hundred chicks in your life, maybe you will, but it's no lie that the first one you don't forget. She never seems to join that line of chicks you make in dark alleys, eat out on dirty stairways, bang in the backs of Buicks. She is, you can't help it, special. For Monterose she was little Irene, Irene with the crazy blue eyes. A spade chick with blue eyes—dig it, it's special. He used to love Irene so badly that each time he was away from her he'd think of nothing but getting back with her saying, "I do love you, J.R. How could I ever love anybody else?"

He'd do anything to make her happy. Buy her candy, give her flowers, anything. He told her once that if she asked he'd even cut it off and give it to her, and any time she wanted she'd have it right there and could play with it, keep it in her bed like a hot-water bottle in the cool of the night. As long as he could emboss his name, even just his initials, on it, so she wouldn't forget it was his. She didn't say, "J.R., you're crazy, I'd never do a thing like that"; instead she looked at him thoughtfully with her big blues and said, "Maybe you better not talk like that, Jerrold. Someday I may have to test you."

And of course you know she did. For when Calvin put the finger on J.R. for his Warlord, he said he'd give him just one test to be sure he had the stuff. They would go to a tailor shop run by a little Jew named Finklestein. Little Mr. bald Finklestein with the hard head. Calvin would go with him, but J.R. would pull the job. He'd have to smack Finklestein over the head—not kill him, just give him a bang he wouldn't forget. And then they'd dip their fingers into the blood, put them together, and pledge a partnership: Calvin the Overlord, J.R. the Warlord. So they went, on a winter night where you break off a nun's titty and suck on it like an icicle, just as Finklestein was closing up. Monterose hit him, but he just groaned. Calvin shouted, "Hit him again, motherfucker, hit him again!" But J.R. froze, his stomach tried to come out of his mouth, and Calvin grabbed the pipe and did it himself. When they got back to the Dragons, he didn't tell the others what had happened. No, he had a better plan. He said, "Oh yeah, J.R.'s my man. He just about killed the mocky cat." So Monterose was made the Warlord, with the top floor of Horror House for his private pad. But Calvin told Irene, only Irene, and soon she was in his bed every night, directly under Monterose. The floor was like Kleenex and Calvin would talk through it to J.R.: "Hey, baby, how you making it? Irene, say something to J.R. He must be awful lonely by himself." And Irene: "Jerrold, I could bring you up some of this ham if you like." And she'd walk up the steps in her little nightgown with a sandwich on a plate, and she'd watch him until he choked on the last bite. "Was it good?" she'd say, and though J.R. imagined each time that she'd fall into his arms, all she gave him was a smile and a swirl of her gown as she headed back to Calvin.

Now on the floor of his old suffering place, then carried down the stairs accompanied by laughter and old-time reminiscing, J.R. dreams:

He is on a beach, very white and warm, made of piles of feathers from exotic birds: eagles, condors, peacocks, egrets. The waves roll in lazily, lush as his mother's body. And everywhere along the shore are pretty chicks in bikinis, ice-cream vendors giving away sundaes, cats playing basketball and volleyball and bouncing in the feathers. J.R. is just a youngster, three feet tall, no big plans except to make the most of the moment. He jumps around in the feathers for a while, then decides to take a dip in that inviting ocean. He is the first one ever to swim there, and he swims out farther than anyone can believe—they shout at him, "Hey kid, where you going? You're going to drown yourself if you keep it up!" But he doesn't listen. He looks down under the green shelf of water, and beneath the waves he sees castles made of emeralds and sapphires nestling in a valley at the bottom. Dig, he says to himself, dig! That's too much! Finally he decides to swim down and take a closer peep, so he takes a deep breath, tries a surface dive, and heads for the jewel city under the sea.

When he reaches the bottom, J.R. notices that the fish are dressed like people—little girl fish in tight dresses, handsome stud fish with rings on their fins and silver hats—and they walk along the wide boulevards of the city smiling and tipping their hats at each other. After a few moments, a girl goldfish gives him the special eye and stops him in his tracks. "Hi," she says with a bell in her voice. "Like me to show you around?"

"Oh yes, I think that'd be just fine."

Smiling at him all the time, she takes him on a tour of the whole city in the valley with its parks, nightclubs, castles, even ballparks. It's like a holiday. Everybody swims along, kidding around, gabbing their heads off. Nobody seems to work, and J.R. realizes he hasn't seen a single cop. "Miss," he says, "you don't mind if I throw you a few questions?"

"Go right ahead."

"Well then," he says, "how come you don't have no cops here?"

She laughs gently, and her smile makes J.R.'s heart turn over. "There's no reason to have police here! Nobody does anything wrong, of course. We do have a little trouble from the turtles, but they come once every ten years, and anyway, we have ways of handling them."

"But don't you even work?"

"Work? Heavens no! Why should we work? What good would that do? Actually, there's only one thing we have to do. Want me to show you?"

She leads him into the largest castle of the city, built from one solid diamond. Inside the glare is so blinding they both slip on shades and walk through rooms where the light bounces from wall to wall in endless variations. When they arrive at the center, J.R. sees ten burly fish standing with spears, guarding two golden cables. "You see," his lady friend says, "all we have to do is watch these cables. They're the ones that keep the world together. You know those lines that go all around the globe?"

"You mean the longitudes and latitudes?"

"That's it. Well, here they are. We have to protect them from anyone who might want to cut them and make the world fall apart."

"Oh Miss," says J.R., "you must be putting me on. Everybody knows that those lines are imaginary."

"Then everybody must be wrong." He knows in an instant that everybody is.

Suddenly he finds himself coming out of the sea. He stands very straight and dignified, and when he touches himself he sees that he is wearing a golden suit. What's more, he knows he has a mission: to protect those fish and keep the world from falling apart. Now all the studs and chicks on the beach look at him differently, for he is six feet six and wearing his golden suit. "Hey, J.R., where did you get that groovy suit?" "J.R. baby, you must be into some fine bread to buy a suit like that!" "Oh, J.R., you look so sexy now!"

"Okay, okay," says J.R. as they crowd around him. "One at a time! Don't push! Everybody'll get a peek. But keep your nasty meathooks off the gabardine. And remember, J.R.'s the big boss from now on. Your friend J.R. is the King."

Through the cheering crowd Calvin comes riding. Lightning is shooting from his eyes. He's seated on a hulking turtle huge as an elephant. J.R. smiles to himself: you just gave yourself away, Calvin baby. I'm hip to which side you're on. But Irene sits in Calvin's lap, and he plays with her titties, the tips stiff as two knives. "What's happening here?" Calvin says, and the fans shout up to him, "It's J.R. He's wearing a golden suit and he's the new King."

"Oh, yeah? We had better take a look."

The crowd parts to let Calvin see. J.R. stretches himself a foot taller, but Calvin still sits above him. There's going to be trouble, J.R. realizes, but he remembers his responsibility to the fish-world.

"Dig, my friend," Calvin says, scratching his chin. "They tell me you got a nice piece of cloth on your shanks. Where might you have copped it?"

"Just around, Calvin baby, just around."

"Well, J.R., you must be around in some places I'm not hip to. Wouldn't you say that?"

"Could be, Calvin. Maybe you're not as foxy as you thought you were."

Calvin leans forward to see better. "That's the way it looks from here." The turtle snorts, and Calvin whispers something to Irene. "Yeah, baby, maybe you better sound him a little," he says, just loud enough for J.R. to hear, and she descends from the turtle, slips up to J.R. and puts her arms around him. "I missed you, J.R. I really did." J.R. sees Calvin sniffing at the air.

"I bet you did. But you're missing me more right now, aren't you, Irene?"

"That's a pretty suit, J.R."

"It's okay."

"It's the nicest suit I've ever seen."

"I guess it might just be, Irene. And the nicest you're ever going to see."

"Remember, J.R., once you said you'd give me something very personal if I wanted it? The thing you treasured most in the world? Well, I wouldn't ask for that, J.R. All I want is your golden suit. Honey, would you give it to me?" She comes closer to him and puts her cool hands on his neck. "Please, J.R., just your golden suit."

J.R. knows he is going to say it, but he can't help himself. "I can't give it to you even if I wanted to. It's not mine. It belongs to the fish—" J.R. has said it, and now the sky turns black and thunder crashes against the sea. Calvin is a hundred feet tall; armies of turtles mass around him. His voice booms out like falling buildings: "THAT'S ALL WE WANTED TO KNOW, MY FRIEND! THAT'S ALL WE WANTED TO KNOW!"

As Calvin and his turtles charge into the sea, J.R. is three feet tall again and stands with the golden suit torn to shreds on the rocky beach.

Monterose is awakened by the harsh morning sun stabbing under his eyelids. He finds himself in the middle of the empty lot in front of Horror House. He wipes the crusts of blood from his scalp and looks at Horror House for the last time. Okay Calvin, he thinks. That's all *I* wanted to know. The world doesn't change, and you don't change it. All you can do is know when it's time to split. Then you look for something better.

Standing tall in his golden suit, he walks down the avenue into the park without looking back.

John Bart Gerald

When She Came Home

All I could think of was Liberty. I tried to push her away
but she was at my fingertips, playing through my mind like
a child teasing me, burning through my body, consuming
all other thoughts, hiding in every closet I turned to hide in,
waiting around every corner, a voice whispering over my
shoulder, and I heard things she said in the dark, I remembered things we wanted together. And they hurt me.
We didn't have them.

It was raining again. Everything was wrong. Liberty
was coming down with a cold. She had left her umbrella on
a bus and her raincoat absorbed water like a sponge. I
looked out at the rain, heard it pouring through the gutters,
tried to let the rain wash her away, clear my head, put out
the fire. I don't know what I wanted from her. I began to
walk the kitchen, trying to think about my work, but she
wouldn't leave me alone. I was afraid I cared more for her
than my own work, more than for my own tricky soul. I
began to bite my fingernails. Caring too much for her put
me on my knees and raised her, gave her wings: she flew.

Then she came home. She came home strong. She
burst through the door with her eyes lit up but cagey,

JOHN BART GERALD has appeared in the *Best American Short
Stories, 1969* and *1970*. This is a chapter from *Hooker's Love
Song,* an unpublished novel.

checking that everything was the same between us. She shut the door, smiling. Her shoes were fish, but most of her coat was dry, only dappled with rain on the shoulders. Some drops trickled down her cheeks along smile lines and dripped off her chin. She looked happy.

"Who walked you home?" I said.

"Louie, to the corner."

"Out of his way."

She came over and tried to change my mouth with her fingers before she bent and licked my lips. Her lips and fingers were cool, articulate, soothing.

I pointed out she was dripping on my manuscripts. She grinned, gathering a handful of her hair and wringing it out over my empty page so two drops of water fell on that letter to no one. Then she brushed my nose with the hair like a paint brush. I tried to grab her, she slipped away, went into the bedroom and changed into my robe and slippers.

She cooked supper. She moved from refrigerator to stove, bent to light the burner and slapped our supper into the black frying pan, talking with her body, cooing, making our usual mess of chili.

When she set our meal on the table her smell mingling with deodorant caught the fumes of cooked red beans. "Come and eat," she said. She watched me eat. I looked back at her hands, her eyes embarrassed me. She breathed with her mouth open because of the cold, the robe rose and sank toward her plate.

"You had a bad day," she said. She searched my face, down my body, my thighs. When I was depressed she was good with me. Her hand touched my shoulder, her palm moved on my arm. "Baby," she said, down deep in her throat.

I know. I know. But I didn't push her hand away. At times Liberty said something to me and it drove a stake into my heart. I knew what the word meant to her, and it cut into me many ways at once. I thought of taking a long walk to get away from her but outside it was still raining.

So I ate the rest of my food. It didn't touch my hunger. Her hand bunched the muscle of my shoulder and left. She was silent now with her absolute sureness, smiling at me with some amusing secret. Her legs crossed, swung back and forth nearing me and departing like a pendulum, with each stroke drawing us nearer the moment when nothing could keep us apart.

I wanted to take her by the shoulders and shake her and say, "Look, woman, I'm nothing right now. I'm no one. I don't have anything to give you. I'm scared and you can't help me." I sat there studying my thumb.

She rattled and washed the dishes in the warm secure world of our home at night where the greatest threat was cockroaches, where we lay side by side night after night silently sharing our secrets and each other. The bathwater muffled the sound of rain pouring through the gutters. The whole city was being cleansed. The tin bath cover leaned against the door. The tub was perched by the sink on its metal legs like a woman holding out her apron. Liberty pinned up her hair. She slipped off her things from under her robe and put them beside me on the table for dessert. Her hand came under my jaw and raised my face to look at her. I stared at the white wedge of her throat. Her fingers left hot prints on my cheek, her hands moved to the collar of her robe. She slipped off the robe and hung it over my head. I saw brief flashes of her nakedness and then only the blue tent wrapping me in her scent. The water pounding in the tub stopped. I took the robe off my head.

Liberty looked about the same as she always did, naked. She was stepping up into the tub, her breasts like apples, and her whole body fresh snow melting down into the hot water.

She cupped the water and brought it to her shoulders, swept it to her throat. Drops glistened on her back. A lank of hair slipped from its pins and darkened on her neck. Her hands looked smooth and cooling on her own body. She caught me watching and I looked away.

"Won't you catch cold?" I said.

"I already have."

"You want to make it worse?"

"Would you care?" she said.

"I do."

"You'd miss my paycheck," she said, washing and turning her arms.

"I was just joking."

"Are you only going to sit there?" she said.

"Do you want me to leave?"

"No, you haven't had a bath for a long time."

"Last week."

"Liar."

I never liked to take baths.

"I'll be all clean for you," she smiled. "And you'll smell like the subway."

"You used to like the way I smelled."

She knelt in the water with splashing and drops of water catching light all over her skin. "Can you get me a towel?"

So I left her to finish and went into the bedroom, found the towel, and when I came back she rose up in the tub pouring water like some sweet syrup. She held out her hand. Ten feet away I stopped and said "Catch."

She caught. Her breasts juggled my soul. She wrapped, tucking the towel between and stepped out onto the floor.

"Your turn," padding toward me wet footprints. "You'll have to bathe alone."

"It won't do any good," I said.

"Feeling sorry for yourself?" She began unbuttoning my shirt, hands wet with droplets sliding down her arms. I wasn't about to have her undress me. I stripped my clothes. She watched me closely. I turned away. She began to fold my clothes and lay them on the chair. My legs were thinning. On the side away from her I took a fist of my haunch, slacker than I remembered, my arm muscles were running mice instead of city rats under the skin. My true self was too docile to be on display. I covered with my hands and shuffled over to the bathtub and climbed in warm splashes.

For an instant I hoped the water would change me. I scrunched down into the warmth, put my head on the bathtub rim and stared at the paint peeling on our ceiling.

Waves of slow breathing rippled on my neck and knees. I stirred like objects under a murky river.

She was roughing herself with a towel.

Out the window rain pattered the roof, tippling into the tin gutters, clogging the drains, the rain washing the city air, my home, a cold rain. The hair on my chest released little bubbles.

Liberty mottled pink and white took the pins out of her hair.

"You better," I said softly, "cover up."

She didn't, she came over against the rim of the tub, red tipped with her long black hair parting around her. She swayed against the tub. "It's cold," she said. "We should bring in the heater."

She leaned over me. "Not ground hog day yet."

"Stop," I said. Her hair ends dangled in my face. I was with some effort up to my chin in water trying to hide under the layer of soap bubbles and former dry skin. I couldn't move without rising in some way to meet her.

"Want me to wash you?" she said.

"No."

"Where are you hiding the soap?" She reached into the water, grappled and found where it was on her own. She began to rub my knees.

"Honey," I fended her off.

This delighted her.

But I had my pride.

"What are you worried about?" she said.

I wasn't sure. So I lay there and she washed me, my knees, my legs, my calloused feet, my chest, my shoulders, and arms, my back. . . . Her hands soothed the water into my skin, passed over me in a clean swathe taking the barnacles off my hull.

I was ready to fall asleep when with one arm holding back her hair she bent and kissed me roughly with her tongue, a long kiss and when she broke off my hands followed her until she was out of reach.

She stood tall over me, smiling again.

"Why?" I said, for I wasn't at my best in the bathtub.

She shrugged, smiling. Her eyes stayed on mine.

I didn't understand her, how she could want me when I was acting like a kid.

"Baby," she said. Like white doves her hands settled and held me.

"Don't call me that."

"What would you like?" Her hands slipped down in the water. It welled up into a wave splashing us. "Sweet baby," she murmured. Her smile was an angel's. I was in anguish. Her fingers were leeches. I lay in her hands, surrounded, vulnerable, needing her. I had no choice. She left me no pretensions.

I wondered how she knew things I couldn't remember teaching her. I reached for her shoulders and pulled her down toward me for a wet kiss until with a slow rending like the tearing of skin she pulled her mouth away. She watched, tense, white teeth, red lip, breathing like she had asthma.

I pulled the plug. I stood up and climbed out on the boards, branded with desire, and ignoring it. Liberty smiled. My face was red and I blazed. I expected the water to steam off my body. She came and wrapped my shoulders with the towel. Her fingers curled up into the hair on my chest. I took the towel and tried to cover myself. I still had to brush my teeth. At the sink the toothpaste looped off the bristles. My legs were not steady after the hot bath. And I wouldn't have minded if she was nibbling my shoulder seriously or if I could have trusted the depth of her breathings but I suspected she was mocking a more passionate woman because she knew it worked on me. I turned around and stomped off toward the light switch but she held on to the towel. I backed bare into the refrigerator, fingered the light switch and let the room fall black. So I went safely into bed.

I heard her feet pattering behind me. I fell on the bed and waited, pointing to the stars like a church steeple. Blood thumped in my ears like the clapper of a great bell stroking the hour. I was confused by wanting when I had nothing to give, nothing to prove. My blood was bellowing for her.

146

"Are you going to say I haven't played fair?" she said.
"No."

She settled on the bed beside me, her hands found my arms and followed them over my head, clasping my wrists against the pillow. She sat in the cold without moving until she said, "Did you say your prayers?"

I wasn't sure whether she was teasing me. I hadn't said my prayers. I should have. God bless all my old friends and Liberty's mother. Make me better every day amen. I pressed my knee against her side. God make me kinder and more like other people. Open my heart even if You have to break it open, so I can love. I'm growing older. When I opened my eyes her hair ends caught in my lashes.

"And did you bless me?" she said, but she didn't wait for an answer. She had her own way of praying with her eyes open. Maybe she prayed all the time. Her flesh pressed down over me. She explored. My pride was tucked away and if I couldn't take her as a man or an artist, I could take her as a child. Her hand offered the apple, her arm encircled my head. And muttering a prayer of the flesh with my lips I gave up for the moment most of the years of my life.

I touched the corners of her mouth, she was smiling. I thought eat and you will be filled, drink and you won't thirst any more. Only it wasn't enough. I was an impostor. I was too old. I had caused too much harm to find ease at her breast. Immersed in her body I couldn't lose myself, the limits of her nakedness were a wall.

So I started off to find what I wanted. My hands groped for a chink in the wall, drawn on by her hands and hips and sounds. I asked and followed her call like a wanderer through carcasses of charred smoldering mattresses, past cars set up on orange crates with their wheels missing, down canyons where rusting fire escapes stuck from the walls, pavement sparkling with bottlecaps and pieces of tinfoil, red beacon turning on a police car, red flowers opening in a window box, cool alleys where lovers hide in the summer, the smell of vinegar, and blue sky up through the girders of a new building.

And all the girls in the city were Liberty, women

I hadn't met, in the backs of tenements, standing in high windows, pressed close in the subway, fragments of her as she opened a door in my heart. Under me her nakedness shed like veils, spreading transparent shower curtains on the air, shuddering as she let each fall from her until bare and quick she grasped my hands.

I swung her around. I pulled her after me. We were running naked through the streets. We were a couple of kids in the playground where I grew up, tangled in the jungle gym, strung out on the cool bars, pushing and riding the swings too high, balancing our hearts with the seesaw while grains from the sandpile drifted through our bodies.

Though it couldn't have been like that, married over six years. My flesh thudded against hers, our sweat smacked of reality. The intake of breath with each moment passed like heart beats, the ticking of the clock, even if we were passing toward something happier than death, gulped like a drink of water. Playgrounds were for kids. We weren't so young. We didn't play any more, how could we? She was too beautiful just for pleasure. On the street I saw how young the mothers looked, the girls with children. I saw Liberty looking out the window fidgeting, her arms empty. I couldn't forget what it was all about. I tried to forget about children, pleasure wasn't play, it was work to forget. And the feeling which had played tag with me all night, maybe all my life, caught up with me again as if some memory were there crying to be recognized, waiting to be made flesh, and I had a sack over my head. There was no break in the wall around myself. Glimpses of beautiful things showed beyond my reach. Maybe what I lacked I was born without. I thought I'd never find it. I was dead sure I could never love.

Well Harry, if you don't, at least you can see that other people make it there, I thought. And for an instant I really did care for her, I was plugging into a light socket, and all her wants and needs and sadness poured over me. I had a moment's glimpse of what it was like to be married to me.

She sensed the change as up at her mother's the cows would smell a storm gathering and all lie down. She started calling for me, and I answered, and gave what she wanted and more. The more I cared the stronger longing came over me, the hope and longing that life would go better, spring would come, giving up to hope like stepping into the blast from a fire-hydrant on a summer day. The longing took root in my body so strong I gathered her up in my arms and leapt off into a burst of lunch-hour sirens, diesel horns, fuses blowing on the big board, folk songs, and a high wind whistling through water tanks on the roof.

Somewhere on the way down I was thinking of my parents.

"Let's get married again," she said. "Start over and do it right."

"We ought to have some kids, Liberty."

She didn't like to talk about it.

"Honey," I said.

"Don't tease me yet, Harry."

"I mean it."

We listened to the rain in the drainpipes.

I was struck by a disturbing thought. "You do still want a kid?'

Her fingers came up and poked my face, forming on my lips and eyelids as though she was blind or deaf, words catching in her throat, and she started to cry, one or two painful catches at first, breaking down into long sobs as a woman gives over again in a love match, opening into laughter or weeping with relief lifting her whole body, smoothing my cheek back time after time as if she was soothing away tears there and I was the one who was crying.

An Interview with
Ishmael Reed
[August 1968]

Conducted and edited by Walt Sheppard,
publisher, *Syracuse Nickel Review.*

When State Magicians Fail

In your novel The Free-Lance Pallbearers *the antagonist
receives deathbed advice, "It's a cruel, cruel world, and
you gots to be swift." How applicable is this advice to the
black writer today?*

The woman giving the advice is like a Mae West in hard
times; this is the kind of figure I wanted to create. I used
long play records, I used television, I used the gothic novel.
It's like a HooDoo-DaDa book, like a collage. All the dumb
white critics who tried to write about the book said, "Well,
duh, Burroughs did the masterprint." I'm not into Burroughs.

I think Burroughs is hung-up on a couple of issues,
just like the whole generation of writers around him. He's
hung-up on a plant. Out of all the millions and millions

ISHMAEL REED is the author of *The Free-Lance Pallbearers* and
Yellow Back Radio Broke Down.

of beautiful plants in the world, why should someone be preoccupied with one plant? That was a '50's movement, a movement of racist writers that the white critics called the Beat Movement. They sucked all the magic, and robbed all the beautiful imaginative ideas from the Negro's brain, turning the Negro into a zombie Bob Kaufman, a great man, a great writer, always overlooked. He did jazz poetry way before those people, they all robbed from him.

Then they tried to become the white Chinamen, and the last I heard, this group of vampires, hustlers, promoters, mediocre people, derivative poets, lowdown dirty robbers and bandits were trying to fool around with the poor American Indian.

The white critics say it was Burroughs. But if you look at Burroughs' books, they're like committee books. You look at *Ticket That Exploded.* The most interesting chapter in the book is the one done by Brion Gysin, a painter. He used the collage method.

My book has more in common with Charles W. Chesnutt in *The Goophered Grapevine.* The critics can't get to that because they've never read an Afro-American novel written before those books that James Baldwin wrote, that Sol Yurick could have written, that Malamud could have written, that Saul Bellow could have written, that Norman Mailer could have written. A whole lot of Jewish writers in New York could have written those books.

I know a whole lot of people who run around the country with their beards and dashikis, with all their Cotton Mather—Aimee Semple McPherson—Billy Sunday philosophy, that think they are Africans. They run around the country saying black writers should be doing new things while the cats who are doing new things, who are really being original, don't have the money to fly around from coast to coast with some committee trying to embezzle honkies, as the terminology goes, and devils, as the terminology goes. And incidentally, this is one thing I want to bring up here: the idea of the devil, this polarization, this two valued schizoid philosophy is Western.

The devil was created by Fourth Century Christian

writers. You don't find the devil in any African system that I know of, because the African systems are pantheistic. Leopold Senghor, Jomo Kenyatta, Kwame Nkrumah are worldly people, they're widely traveled, they're above all that. So what I'm saying is that these people who fly around from coast to coast talking about the black artist ought to create a new form, ought to stay home sometime and try to come up with a new form. I think I've come up with a new form.

We live in a time when a writer can be influenced by all kinds of media. You can pick it up from TV, you don't have to read a single book. So to get back to the question, that character was used to state a pragmatic philosophy in a vaudevillian way. I consider the book not a novel but a vaudeville show. I think it comes out of minstrelsy, like Bert Williams, who many have said was a better comedian than W.C. Fields. In my novel I have tried to utilize pulp form, popular American forms, mass cult, kitsch, as they call it. Like my own experience growing up in Buffalo, N.Y.—the skyline of Buffalo, N.Y. looks like the *Reader's Digest*. They've got a City Hall that's like pop-neo Al Capp-Indian-Polish, that's the architecture. And these guys sit around using double negatives, buttoning the third button on their suit coats; they're the leaders.

You don't have to go to Europe; living in an American city is an art form. You take Cazenovia, New York, where we're having this conference. They should take Cazenovia, New York, dismantle it, and put it in the Whitney Museum. It would put Warhol out of business. Just living in America is like being into a new thing that no one's ever been into before. These are the forms I use in *Pallbearers*. That woman-figure, she's a hard bitchy chick. It's like the only line that was deleted from my book: "The fumes from her broken snatch filled the alley." I'm not beating around the bush like using Lilith eating apples, or Eve, I'm running it right down front. Where did Mae West come from? In all her films she's picking up on the black thing, just like Janis Joplin. Janis Joplin ought to devote 15 percent of her wages to a museum for Bessie Smith.

All these groups like Vanilla Fudge, Cream, show the white supremacy in rock 'n' roll. The so-called Underground Acid Rock stations don't play black people. The only time I heard black blues played in San Francisco was when the disc jockeys were women. Now what's that all about? The Fugs got their title from Red Foxx, but I've never seen them admit that. I've had my experience with racism all over. For instance, I founded the *East Village Other*. Me and one other cat set up the dummy, and I hired the present managing editor. And I named the newspaper. The vampires who robbed all that don't even know what the name means. I got it from a book of criticism on *Paradise Lost* by Jung. He mentioned the "other" as a devil. It stands for a whole generation, we're the others, we're the outsiders.

Like the book *Pallbearers* is a collage of American experience. It has nothing to do with Burroughs. The only good criticism I saw compared it to Hieronymus Bosch. I can dig that because it's the Middle Ages, and I'm a peasant like Hieronymus Bosch. And what comes after the Middle Ages? A Renaissance. That's what's happening right now, but nobody can get to it. Like the peasants come out of strange places, peasants who have never even gone ten blocks are going to incorporate the whole experience and find out where everybody's at. The old institutions are dying.

The question has arisen recently, among black writers, as to whom they should be writing for. Eldridge Cleaver criticizes Baldwin for writing only for white people, and recently William Melvin Kelly stated that from now on he will be writing only for black people. Whom do you write for?

William Melvin Kelly is a fine artist. I think the Afro-American artist should have as much freedom as anybody else. I haven't seen J.D. Salinger in years. Clifford Still doesn't even come out of his house. The Afro-American artist is in a deep and severe crisis from all these people who go around using terms like "cultural revolution." Cultural revolution is something they took from the so-called third world. How does Mao treat his writers and artists? I know everybody digs all the campy clichés in the *Little Red Book,* but I would say that a cat who wants people to go off and say his name over and over again for four hours, when they could be home doing their own thing, must have the most grotesque personality problem in history. That's why I'm an anarchist.

Eldridge Cleaver is a nice guy, a regular fellow; I'd like to play checkers with him some time. William Melvin Kelly is a fine artist. He ought to do his own thing and forget about all those creeps who hold conferences talking about what the writer should do, when the real writers are home writing; what the artist should do, when the real artists are home painting; what the musician should do, when the real musician is home composing. Black people don't need anybody telling them what we should do, where we should eat, how we should act, who we should sleep with. That's like the same old goon squad, the same old HARRY SAM I tried to create in my novel, a dictatorship from the mediocrity. And the only thing that keeps the creeps in business is a sick white media.

I've seen a lot of white people, really beautiful people, who resist LBJ and HHH, but believe that fascism is good for everybody else.

You mentioned the concept of resistance. One aspect of resistance that black militants usually avoid mentioning these days is the kind that seems to have predominated during the slave times: breaking tools, using songs to communicate plots, and utilizing the stereotype to beat the master out of something. Is this aspect of resistance applicable to the present resistance movement, especially among black artists?

If you look at the debates between W.E.B. DuBois and Booker T. Washington, or look at Marcus Garvey, there was always dissent within the movement. That's why I dig

Harold Cruse so much. Everybody ought to read his book *Crisis of the Negro Intellectual*, and Steve Cannon, whose book is being brought out by Random House. This is a new movement. We don't want fascism. We don't want some goon in a black leather jacket telling us what to do when he is going to end up beating on his own people, but grin before the white media. The artists will function as they will. Ralph Ellison, William Melvin Kelly, Charles Wright, Bob Kaufman are all great artists; they're helping the movement a lot more than some of the Black Power people, some of whom are even besmirching the name of Malcolm X because he's dead and can't defend himself.

Malcolm X was a universalist, a humanist and a global man. He was in a position to lead the people of this planet. This tribalism is for the birds. Tribalism dates back to thousands of years ago when people didn't see nobody for days. With technology, tribalism and separatism are impossible. Given communications satellites, computers, international rapid transit, etc., you *can't* be a separatist. Malcolm X was way beyond all that. That's why he got shot. That's why King got killed. Once you become an international mind-miner it's all over. That's where the Afro-American artist is today: John Coltrane going to Ali Akbar Khan, Afro-American ragas, Bill Dixon doing science-fiction music, Sun Ra into Gustav Holst.

Your novel has been called satire, has been compared stylistically with a Swiftian approach. But upon reading, it seems that the novel would be easily recognizable by a cat on the corner of any ghetto street as "the way it is." Why have the critics treated it only on the level of satire?

Because they're scared of a Renaissance. Fortunately the novel got enough support so that I could appeal to the planet; I didn't have to appeal to any particular group. The critics, who are politically aligned, like to promote their girl friends, their boy friends, the guy they went yachting with last Saturday. In a period of, I don't want to use the word decadence because I don't believe in this organic reading of culture—I know a lot of people who should know better going around like the bearded 42nd Street cat saying "Repent"—I think America's going through a very unpleasant interlude. America was set up as an experiment by some very groovy people. Jefferson was a blind racist, but on many other matters he was very correct. If Jefferson was around today, he'd be wearing love beads, reading Peace Eye Book Store and Eldridge Cleaver, looking all over for information.

Then there was Alexander Hamilton, the Negro, the Afro-American. People try to deny that he was black, but it just so happens that I dug up and photostated a miscegenation suit that they put on him. Now if he was white, why would they put that on him? If you look back, Thomas Jefferson always treated him like a nigger. Alexander Hamilton came from the West Indies. He was black, and Aaron Burr shot him because they were jealous of him because he was so tricky and groovy with the women. This is the cat that put the Constitution together. This is the cat that set up the bank.

So I'm not into this "decline and fall"; I'm not into that kind of thing. The critics are afraid because for them this is a trying period. Anglo-Saxons dominated this literature for a long time and wouldn't even recognize fellow Anglo-Saxons who were trying to talk about America. Like Roger Williams going out and talking to the Indians, trying to see what the Algonquins were into. They couldn't dig Mark Twain, they couldn't dig Stephen Crane, they couldn't dig their own people. I found that out at this conference. I'm supposed to be interested in Afro-American writers, but I just introduced about thirty white writers they don't even know about.

The critics are afraid that the black people will have a Renaissance and they will break out of this exotic zoo that critics have put them in: one novelist, one playwright, one poet, one opera singer, one mathematician, one scientist, one astronaut. And if they break out of the exotic zoo, and the floodgates open, then what you have is something they can't deal with. I understand where they're at, I sympathize with them.

I'm not bitter about the Sunday *New York Times* refusing to review my work, just because I had Irving Goosman, the mad slum lord, in there. But Sol Yurick can put down black people, Al Jolson can paint himself blackface, Mailer in *An American Dream* can have a stereotyped racist attitude towards the black man—Shago Martin pulls a switchblade on people—all the stereotypes. Norman Mailer can get away with that. But when a black man tries to be a satirist, tries to look at the whole universe, *The New York Review of Books,* Jason Epstein, the *New York Times,* all these cats get uptight. These people should resign if they're trying to approach art from extra-artistic considerations. You see that's not fair; that's not in the game.

It just so happens that I have such a grass-roots thing that they can't do nothing. Criticism in America reflects the society—the business, the military, the Pentagon. The critics are whores. I sympathize with them; that's something for them to live with; that's their conscience. If I was in their position I would be scared every time a doorknob turned, every time I heard a bump in the night I'd be very upset. But that's their problem. I understand their wives are probably running around on them and they live very groovy lives. That's why they dig Herzog so much, because the critics identify with Herzog—I got a girl friend around the corner. I write letters to the *New York Times,* I got just a little bit of cancer—that's their whole syndrome.

But that has nothing to do with what's happening in America. What's happening in America is people from coast to coast—white, black, Indian, everything else—are writing poems. And the critics say "Duh, is it Art?" But they keep on writing poems, and they're doing music. They're carrying on like the brave cats in France, the surrealists, and the Dadaists. Their only mistake was that they treated it as art and tried to keep it in the salon. But when it comes to America it becomes a mimeographed magazine, it becomes a newspaper, like your newspaper, it becomes like an art form. What surrealism, Dadaism, do in America is you get groovy people like yourself and your photographers, people working with you, who see America and all its forms as art. And when that happens it's all over. Like the Pentagon Demonstration.

The whole idea is when state magicians fail, unofficial magicians become stronger. That's what's happening. But all that stuff Cleaver did in his book was done before by Calvin Hernton who was hounded out of the country for daring to say what the so-called race problem was all about. James Baldwin is an easy target. Nobody takes James Baldwin seriously any more except Jewish liberals. I mean, why should anybody be using the machinery of the *Book of Genesis* when it's been done before? You can't match the *Book of Genesis* or *The Old Testament*. The cats who did that were freaky and psychedelic, hermits and outcasts. That was another century. If you want to talk about this time, you have to come up with new myths, like what Jung calls autochthonous myths. That's what I'm trying to do.

I'm not flying around the country in a dashiki talking about what I'm going to do; I'm trying to do it just like Cecil Taylor's trying to do it, just like Bill Dixon's trying to do it, just like Sun Ra's trying to do it. Slowly, alone, just like Coltrane tried to do it, just like A.B. Spellman tries to do it, just like Bob Kaufman tried to do it. Bob Kaufman didn't have a mob going to bed with him, he didn't get up with a whole lot of company. He had to do it alone. You can talk all you want about what the artist should do, what the artist shouldn't do, 'til the cows come home ding-donging their bells through the pastures. But the Afro-American artist today is an international mind-miner. He's synchrotistic already. He's Afro, he's American, and if he goes to India and does a raga, he's Afro-American-Indian. He's a space cadet, and if you try to put him in a bag you're being dishonest.

I accuse some of these people who have led a whole group of black people astray of intellectual dishonesty bordering on criminal proportions. It's not a game. People have died in the streets clutching unredeemable coupons and refuse from ugly shop windows.

Now when you get out there and put yourself on the media, you have to understand that people like CBS are interested in show-business. I got kicked off CBS for saying that, because before I went on CBS I read *Due to Circumstances Beyond Our Control* by Fred Friendly. Every so-called militant with a duck soup on his head and an ankh around his neck, which he doesn't know the meaning of, ought to read that book. Fred Friendly and cats like Edward R. Murrow were liberals, but they paid dues. When Edward R. Murrow died they had to have bodyguards follow his children around because of what he did on TV. Those cats were the underground press of their time. Friendly says the cats that do the six o'clock got their backgrounds in show-business and vaudeville. They're not interested in news. They say "Da-da-da-da-dum-de-dum. Show-business. Bring on the niggers. OK, five minutes, niggers, come on. Bring on the gooks. Five minutes, gooks." And the niggers and gooks don't even get flowers for their performance when their act has been leaving them in the aisles for five years. I think we've got a little treason trial coming up. I think we've got a few people who owe us an explanation as to what's been going down.

So I don't even know if it's necessary to have critics. Although that cat that did the criticism of *Pallbearers* for you, that cat has a future. I think the critics operate out of a formula: you compare a living writer with ten dead writers and three contemporaries. Alain Robbe-Grillet, in *The New Novel,* says that if you say a man writes like Flaubert, that means you are living in Flaubert's time and doing something that Flaubert did infinitely better.

We don't really need critics because the ancient tradition of Afro-American art is anonymity. Like field chants —we don't know who did "Stagger Lee." In Africa you find art is a function of the society. Like somebody says, "Well damn, I think I'll make myself a groovy plate." He didn't put his name to it. Somebody said, "Well, I think I'll make up this beautiful song to make the day go fast." He didn't sign his name to it. All the critic's terminology is Western anyway. Like role, that's Elizabethan. Aesthetic, that dates back to the time when some European philosopher was laying up in a big mansion all day talking about, "Does time begin in space, or does space begin in time?" We don't even need all that.

John A. Williams, after visiting Africa, writes a warning that the Afro-American artist cannot look to Africa because what he seeks is not there. What does Africa hold for the Afro-American artist?

John Williams wrote a titanic book. What he did was equivalent to what Mahler did with the romantic symphony, taking it to its huge, crashing conclusion. In *The Man Who Cried I Am,* John Williams summed up the Wrightian novel. Some of those people on the David Susskind-telstar-closet queen-freak hour ought to read that book. What can we say about the "King Alfred Plan"? Now that's really interesting. I mean the plan is already out there and they just want a provocation.

I think John Williams is correct about Africa. So many people are trying to put an emphasis on Africa when the fact of the matter is the Africans don't even put an emphasis on Africa. The Ghanaian poets, for example, are very Western. "Négritude" is a French concept. So that we're not even doing what the contemporary Africans are doing. We have so many volumes and volumes of experience here we could keep on going forever. I think that the only reason we neglect them is that we associate them with the bad old days of colonialism, so that we don't think it's worthy, in that way we fall into a white man's bag towards black art. It's the same mistake that whites make when they look to Europe, looking to French or Italian or Russian studies when all the time it's right under your nose.

Look at the American narratives; look at the slave narratives; look at the narratives of the people crossing the

Rocky Mountains in 1821; look at the narratives that came out of the Civil War, written by common people. This may turn out to be the American art form anyway, more than the novel. In fact, the cats who get into this African thing really come on like Edgar Rice Burroughs in reverse. It's what Harold Cruse calls Africanesque. Africans would laugh them out of business. These people talking about black consciousness, after all, are intellectuals who have been chased out of the ghetto because black people don't want to hear it, they know better.

I think that Steve Cannon and Adam David Miller are the most perceptive critics in America because they work hard. They're not out there trying to pull a goon squad aesthetic on black people. They're merely describing what's happening. If black people line up in front of the Apollo Theater, all around the block, to see Amos Milburn or Etta James or James Brown, then maybe that's the consciousness instead of some derivative thing some intellectual read in a book. Much of the thinking of the black intellectual comes from Marxism, and that's not red-baiting, it's the way it happens historically. It's all there in the "Brotherhood" in Ralph Ellison's *Invisible Man,* or in Max in Richard Wright's *Native Son:* "We have no heritage." We do have a heritage. You may think it's scummy and low-down and funky and homespun, but it's there. I think it's beautiful. I'd invite it to dinner. And I think that's what *Pallbearers* is all about.

The reaction to *Pallbearers* was very interesting. Black people off the streets and scholars dug it; no in between. I think it's a cosmic book; that's what I was trying to get into.

John Williams is like a catalyst, like an observer. That's what I get from his books. I don't know him, but he's probably a very reticent man, not garrulous like myself. He's an observer, and from his looks you can tell that he's seen a lot go down. He's got ten years on my generation and I'd like to see how he saw it. He's right about this "See what's in your house first before you go outside."

You've spoken of a Renaissance, McLuhan, pulp art, the "others," the rise of the "unofficial magicians." Where is all this leading us?

First, I think we will appreciably curtail Judeo-Christian culture's domination of our senses. I think we're doing it now, and I think we've been successful so far. People operate on a very common level of experience; they can only deal with the very obvious. I think the readers of your paper ought to analyze the Pentagon Demonstration very carefully. Because that was the first time that HooDooism, agit-prop, Dada, surrealism have been utilized, like the idea of levitating the Pentagon. What's ahead, I think, is that this system is going to fall, probably through a bloodless coup. It's already a bloodless coup when the old whiskey drinkers who run the country are stumbling around like Frankenstein.

What we're going to see emerge is a cooperative of autonomous groups who are going to come up with new ways of making America work, thus making the planet work. We're already seeing that the old religious institutions are dying and they die hard. Look at Czechoslovakia, which has the largest so-called hippie community in the world. They started doing really desirable things, but Big Brother didn't like it so he sent in the tanks. Just like this creep over here sends the tanks in—that's their only solution.

But we're in a position now that when spirit and imagination enter the streets, that's the ball game. The '70's will belong to black people, Indians, cosmic creatures and anybody else who wants to climb aboard.